The Vanishing Island and Other Stories

Alex M. Castillo

Ukiyoto Publishing

All global publishing rights are held by

Ukiyoto Publishing

Published in 2024

Content Copyright © Alex M. Castillo

ISBN 9789364941075

All rights reserved.

No part of this publication may be reproduced, transmitted, or stored in a retrieval system, in any form by any means, electronic, mechanical, photocopying, recording or otherwise, without the prior permission of the publisher.

The moral rights of the author have been asserted.

This is a work of fiction. Names, characters, businesses, places, events, locales, and incidents are either the products of the author's imagination or used in a fictitious manner. Any resemblance to actual persons, living or dead, or actual events is purely coincidental.

This book is sold subject to the condition that it shall not by way of trade or otherwise, be lent, resold, hired out or otherwise circulated, without the publisher's prior consent, in any form of binding or cover other than that in which it is published.

www.ukiyoto.com

For my parents Candoy and Luning

Contents

PROLOGUE	1
CHAPTER 1: HOMECOMING	5
Chapter 2: Fiesta!	17
Chapter 3: Son of the Soil	25
Chapter 4: Lost in the woods	36
Chapter 5: Bladed Verses	41
Chapter 6: The Engkantada and Panganahaw	47
Chapter 7: The Storm	51
Chapter 8: Two storms	57
Chapter 9: The Younger Children	60
Chapter 10: Kapidos & Luning	67
Chapter 11: The Vanishing Island	75
Chapter 12: Elma and Elmo	77
Chapter 13: The Tragedy at Sea	82
Chapter 14: Gamblers and Thieves	88
Chapter 15: The Weaver	90
Chapter 16: Harvest Season	92
Chapter 17: Graduation from Elementary	94
Chapter 18: The Second Storm	97
Chapter 19: The Engkantos	107
Chapter 20: The Drought	112
Chapter 21: The Enchanted Island	115
Chapter 22: Leaving the Island for the First Time	119
Chapter 23: The Last Fiesta	126
About the Author	**133**

PROLOGUE

Even from outside, the house looks desolate and lifeless. The San Francisco hedge and other ornamental plants at the front yard are overgrown. Their colorful leaves rustle at the gentle breeze that suddenly sweeps from the ocean and they fleetingly come to life. I gaze at them momentarily as if expecting someone to materialize. The dancing ladies are surprisingly blooming with their bright yellow petals perched on the trunk of the old palm tree at either side of the fence at the main entrance. I am surprised that they bloom even with neglect and they bring the needed life to the otherwise gloomy place. The exposed shelves are what is left of the small store in the left corner of the front porch with a few leftover salt in small plastic bags. I retrieved the key from under the wooden bench and slid it on the lock. The crackling of the rusty chain startles a bat that hurriedly flies out from the gaping hole overhead. I wonder if it could find its way in the noonday sun. Even in the past, we would occasionally find a fruit bat hanging upside down from the awning of the back window so I was not surprised to find the nocturnal animal in the house. I wonder what else found solace in the old house.

The house smells of mildew and other scents of neglect. The furniture is intact in their places saved for the divan that was dragged from its original corner probably to save it from the dripping rain water from a hole in the roof. A shaft of sunlight shines like a spotlight at my college diploma hanging on the wall along with other old family photographs, pictures taken from my previous homecomings and the few times that my older siblings were home for the fiesta. Standing in the middle of the living room, I stared at it for a few minutes, looking at my youthful face, full of optimism and vigor not realizing that my brother was at the door. He must have been informed by somebody that I was home.

I blew the embers in the fireplace trying to revive the kindling that my brother used to boil water for his coffee that morning but the ashes clouded my eyeglasses and scattered on my face.

"The matches are on the overhead shelves. I'll get some firewood if you need to cook something." Dong opened the kitchen door leading to where the comfort room is. "I or the children sometimes sleep here. But nobody really lives here since Nanay died." Mother died two summers back after Tatay died peacefully one July morning before his 80th birthday. It had been an empty nest for our parents after all of us left the family house when our youngest sister opted to live in her husband's village on the western side of the island. Sometimes I would imagine my parents huddling together in the big house like newlyweds sixty years before, thinking about the time when all of us ten living children would be back in the same house, crowding the cramped kitchen during meal times. It was during meal times that Tatay would instruct my older brothers what needed to be done in the farm during the weekend or after school: the weeds needed pulling, another *kaingin* had to be cleared while there was lull in the rice farming after the paddies had been planted. My older sisters and I were tasked to pound rice or grate cassava or sweetpotato to become delicacies that we sold around the village. My mouth waters with the thought of the rice cakes and cassava rolls my mother used to make.

Dong strikes a match and burns some coconut husk to start a fire and adds some kindling. I watch the smoke rise and gather at the thatch roof before escaping at the gaps. Dong filled a pot of fresh water while I retrieved the instant coffee from one of my bags. I filled a plastic bag of coffee, chocolate drink and candies for Dong's children not realizing that his elder children are already teenagers. The house is still as solid as a rock saved for the few holes in the roof. The sky light in the dining room provides much of the natural light. A cool breeze entered the room as I opened the windows and somehow rejuvenated the dank place. The dining table made of Narra needs polishing as well as the two long benches at either side but they are functional and not a foot missing. Nanay and Tatay sat at the opposite ends of it on a single bench while we children sat in our designated places like school children; behaved and made no unnecessary noise.

The rooms are clean but bare. My old clothes are still in the drawers. They smell of moth balls but most of them have gathered dust where they are folded. The pillows have watermarks on them which look like they've been wet from sweat and were not totally dried. They also smell of mold. I checked the other drawers for some pillow cases and saw some clean sheets too so I replaced the old ones. I fished my shorts and sando from one of my bags and sat on the wooden bed and looked around my old room. Nothing much has changed even the books and old magazines stacked on the small table against the wall. My parents' room is also bare, saved for the old curtains hanging at the north window that opens to our neighbor. Their old clothes are still folded on the drawers so I took a mental note to discard some of them, maybe donate the newer ones to some of our relatives.

Dong had informed me that our neighbor at the back asked permission to tap electricity from our house and my siblings agreed to this arrangement to avoid it from being disconnected. They pay for the monthly bill since we consumed very little electricity since nobody lived permanently in the house.

"Are you back for good?" Dong asks while blowing the fire. He is frying some hotdogs that I bought in Matnog while the rice was also cooking on the other stone stove.

"I will stay for a while. I need to sort things out. I will decide after the fiesta if I will stay or not." I mumbled.

I drew water from the open well at the back and filled the earthen jar in the comfort room so I could refresh myself. The open well too is still used by our neighbors and surprisingly, the water level is high enough even in the middle of summer.

"It had been raining regularly since the start of May", Dong remarked. I feel that the dust from the bus ride from Legazpi airport to Matnog port is clinging to my skin so I enjoyed a full bath. Looking around, I can see that the outside bathroom is constantly used but the tin roof needs replacement. The old earthen jar from Tata Bala still sits in the corner as a welcome relic from the past. Suddenly, loud music blared from the plaza to signal the start of the basketball games and I was reminded that the fiesta is only a few days away.

My mother wanted me to become a teacher so I could teach in the village school but I wanted to be something else, something away from the prying eyes at home because I didn't want to limit my choices. I didn't want the small town gaze and the need to explain everything to people that don't even matter to me. In the village, everybody knows everyone's lives to the smallest detail and everyone has an opinion about everyone's decisions.

One year ago, I finally decided to resign from my corporate job and enrolled in a certificate course in education which I have wanted to do for the longest time. The six to eight hours daily commute finally got me aside from the stress of always answering to some corporate god and explaining why the minimum wage workers are leaving for easier minimum wage jobs. I felt that I was slowly losing my soul while witnessing some injustices done to small workers but could not fight it tooth and nail because it was legal anyway. I wanted a change of environment.

Maybe mother was right. I should have stayed and taught on the island.

CHAPTER 1: HOMECOMING

The plane landed on the tarmac of the Legazpi airport at 5:15 a.m. one of the few times that it was on time. I slept most of the one hour flight as soon as I was settled on my seat as I wanted to be awake on the land trip to Matnog Port so I was jolted awake when the plane made a thug upon landing. I peered through the window while the plane was taxiing to the lone terminal. It was a clear summer day. The majestic Mt. Mayon stood guard in the background as the morning sun peeked from the east. When the plane finally stopped, the stewardess announced that we could get up and retrieve our hand-carried bags and filed out on the aisle. My eyes squinted to adjust to the sunlight as I stepped out of the plane.

The horizon was cloudless. Some passengers took photographs of themselves on the tarmac with the iconic perfect-cone volcano that was also one of the most active. Mayon has erupted several times since time immemorial. The ruins of the nearby Cagsawa Church are witness to its fury in the previous century when the whole town of Daraga and nearby towns were almost annihilated during one of its major eruption in 1814. The lava and ash fall covered whole communities along its track and killed thousands of people. Only the belfry of the Cagsawa Church remained standing, which was an indication of a once thriving community. Houses, farms and commercial buildings were buried in several feet of lahar and volcanic rocks that wiped out the whole town of Daraga. In recent memory, in the year 2006, a few months after another major eruption, Typhoon Reming hit Albay province that caused flooding in the towns intensified by lahar flow with volcanic rocks cascading from the slopes to the communities along the rivers that left several hundreds dead. People say it was inferno personified, with fire flowing down to the slopes several miles around the perimeter of the volcano. The devastation was still evident during my homecoming in May the following year; boulders blocked the rivers that traversed the towns leaving houses and farms in feet-deep lahar, but the flowers jutting among the rocks in the paddies were a welcome sight and were a reminder of that vicious life cycle in the shadow of an active volcano. People are used to it now although they are on the lookout of telling signs whenever Mayon would jolt them from their slumbers at any time of the day or night.

From my memory though, Mayon's volcanic eruptions were not always destructive. I was about nine or ten years old when I witnessed the lava flow in one of its minor eruptions in the mid 1980's. It was visible at night time from the top of the hill near our farm house in Sitio Baquiw. My siblings and I watched in awe as Mayon spewed fire into the night sky in slow intervals. It was a magical moment and I imagined the Lady like a dragon breathing fire to its enemies like in fairy tales. Legend has it that the volcano is protected by Daragang Magayon, the lady of the Volcano who is as beautiful as she is ferocious.

Being in the path of typhoons, the Bicol and Samar regions share the same experiences. Since my island town is nestled between the islands of Samar and Luzon, we are in affinity to both islands. Traders and farmers from our island sell their copra in Matnog or Bulan towns in Sorsogon where we also buy fiesta commodities since there are no big grocery stores in Capul. Eventually, young people leave the island to work or study in big cities like Manila or Calbayog and in my case, Tacloban in Leyte. Some choose the state university in the capital town of Catarman which is only two to three hours away. There are daily trips to Matnog port in Luzon and Allen port in Samar from the island so it was normal for people to travel the perilous San Bernardino Strait even on stormy days. When I was in college, I would not miss the Christmas break for anything, even if it meant going home soaking wet from the gigantic waves. There was a time when our boat drifted to the island of San Antonio because of poor visibility due to torrential rains brought by the *amihan* season. We had to dock temporarily in the neighboring island to mend the outrigger that was pushed back by enormous waves. Eventually, we proceeded to another pier in the town of Victoria instead of Allen port. It was a close call and some of us were visibly shaken by the experience. We were covered by tarpaulin as the roof had caved in on us while the crew rushed to pick the broken outriggers to prevent it from being washed away. The engine stopped. Someone prayed aloud The Lord's Prayer while stifling cries. The other crew members stood on opposite sides trying to balance the boat while it was battered by colossal waves while the others tied bamboo poles to mend the broken outrigger. All our bags were soaked so we borrowed a change of clothing from our relatives in Victoria and Tangulon before proceeding to Tacloban. It was not the first nor the last of such horrifying experiences. It is a norm of island life.

I did not leave the island until I was fifteen years old to take the National College Entrance Exam in Allen town. Mother accompanied me and we stayed overnight with my uncle, a medical doctor, at his cottage inside the Allen District Hospital. I was with a few other classmate-cousins with their parents and we crammed the living room as well as the kitchen. I did not speak Waray so when I bought some eggs for breakfast, I spoke Tagalog and the owner thought I was from Manila and spoke in heavily accented Tagalog too. The second and third time was when I took the college entrance examination at the University of the Philippines in Tacloban and later at the University of Eastern Philippines at the provincial capital of Catarman. I passed both examinations and eventually enrolled at UP where I struggled to maintain my scholarship.

My first time in Matnog was when I travelled with my theater group for our tour in Manila and Baguio during my junior year in college. We took the 24-hour bus ride from Tacloban to Manila and just like my first long trip, I tried to stay awake and memorized the names along the Maharlika Highway to match the names and the places that I heard on the radio during typhoons. It was the first trip to Manila for most of us so we were almost inseparable as a group even when buying snacks and other essentials at the convenience store.

Samar and Bicol regions are both located along the path of the annual typhoons. The location of the typhoon was our barometer in gauging its impact to our island town that is located at the southernmost tip of the island of Luzon and the northernmost tip of the main island of Samar. If the typhoon would hit the provinces of Sorsogon and Masbate, it would make a landfall too in Capul. According to the weather bureau, the Philippines experiences 20 to 25 typhoons annually and more than 50% of them hit our island town. The typhoons start coming in as early as June and the strongest come during the ber-months. Sometimes, we experience two typhoons in a month. Old people would recall the strongest one from memory and they would gauge the strength of the latest by the last one that ravaged the island. Damaged crops and coconut plantations are norms after a major typhoon so I had to scrimp on my stipend to get through with college. That would mean fewer harvest for my family so I did not expect them to send me money until the end of the second semester in March.

I hopped on a tricycle after claiming my luggage to take me to the bus terminal and took the first one to depart for Bulan Sorsogon. Unfortunately, there were no direct bus trips to Matnog port and the jeepneys leave a while longer and I had to catch the passenger motorboats that leave a little before noon. The bus stopped briefly at Irosin Terminal to drop off and take more passengers. I took the opportunity to buy candied pili nuts for my mother and young nephews and nieces. I also bought a few canisters for the fruit salad. As the bus speeded along the Maharlika Highway, I marveled at the villages along the road, their activities were in full swing before the sun became too hot. Just like in our village, the farmers were manually harvesting rice with a scythe while the others were drying their harvest on *buri* mats spread along the side roads. Vendors selling candied pili nuts, rice cakes, banana fritters, citrus fruits, boiled eggs and peanuts and bottled waters came aboard whenever the bus stopped to drop off or take more passengers.

In my past homecomings, I would take the overnight bus from Manila to Matnog and would memorize the names of the towns and villages along the Maharlika Highway. Since May is fiesta month, I would count the celebrations that we passed along the way; people converging in the town plaza, dancing until the early morning, the drunk sleeping in some benches or even on the ground while the sound system was blaring the latest dance craze in Manila. Most public plazas were situated along the national highway with a mobile sound system and disco lights strung all around the place. I would crane my neck on the window to take a peek and discovered that they were similar to our celebrations at home. The VIP guests and the politicians are seated at the presidential table together with the local elites while the young lovers seize the opportunity to talk under the shades or when the dance turns "sweet" nostalgic of my own youth.

After another two hours, the bus conductor announced that we were at Barangay Trece, the intersection between Bulan and Matnog towns, so I picked my bags from the overhead bin. The conductor helped me with my bigger bag while I clutched my hand bag and carried my backpack.

Several tricycle drivers offered their services while I alighted. The fare was two hundred pesos because I had no companion to split the fare. The driver secured my luggage at the roof and at the back of his tricycle and then I settled myself inside. The ride was bumpy as we traversed on potholes and unfinished road works so I reminded the driver to slow down in some parts. Every so often, I would reach out for my luggage especially when we navigated the winding road approaching the port of Matnog. It was a good eighteen kilometers from Trece to the port and my ears were ringing from the cacophonous sound of the mufflers long after I arrived in Matnog.

It was almost lunchtime when I reached the port but I had time for a quick lunch at one of the carenderias along the pier. One of the motorboat crew approached me as soon as I got off.

"Do you have other companions?" Nestor asked while taking my bags. I knew him since we were small like I knew everyone in the village.

"No. I am alone. Are we sailing already?" He got all my luggage and carried it to the boat.

". . .In a few minutes. We are waiting for the others to finish their marketing"

The other passengers were starting to get aboard the motorboat while the businessmen were getting their goods loaded ahead. There were other Abaknon passengers waiting at the dock. Some were familiar faces while others were too young for me to remember or were children of vacationing locals. I just nod every time someone greeted me since I could not remember their names. Fiestas are annual exodus for most of us rooted in the island. Most families hold their informal reunions during the fiestas and it is expected that relatives will join them even without a formal invitation. Families prepare a great deal and spend a substantial amount for food even to the extent of asking for loans for this purpose. I was finishing my meal of fish *tinola* when the crew signaled that it was time to sail.

It was high tide. I took off my shoes and rolled up my pants ready to wade in the thigh-deep water but a boy of about eighteen summers offered to carry me on his shoulders.

"Come on, I can carry you". He smiled shyly.

"No, I can wade on the water. . . ."

I know I have gained weight due to my almost deskbound lifestyle in the city but he was already on his knees so I reluctantly planted myself on his broad shoulders. He wobbled a little bit as he got up so I hesitated for a while.

"You know I can wade on the water. . ."

"Your shoes will get wet. Hold on to my head to make yourself steady". He instructed me shyly.

I was still reluctant as I sat on his shoulders, afraid that both of us would stumble to the water but before I could finish my thought, he had planted me firmly on the ramp. I made a quick glance at him as he left to take more passengers. His caramel-colored skin glistened in the midday sun and I caught his boyish smile again as I steadied myself on the ramp of the San Ignacio.

I found a place and sat amongst the other passengers composed of *balikbayans* and merchants. I wanted to check where my bags were but they were already covered with tarpaulin together with the other luggage on the portside. The cases of beer and soft drinks were loaded at the bottom by the starboard.

"How's work? Are you married?" asked the middle-aged lady to my right.

"No, I am not married", I answered curtly. She was familiar but her name skipped me at the moment. She was younger than me but she has aged beyond her years. Her skin was sunburned and her breasts sagged. Her hips were wide and some of her front teeth were missing but she didn't seem to mind as she smiled widely. Her excitement added to her high-pitched voice as she continued talking.

"But you have a stable job. You should already get a wife to take care of you"

I smiled and pretended to check my hand-carried bag and pulled out some wet wipes for my face. My ears were still ringing from the tricycle ride. Luckily, the crew started the engine not before long.

"Uno, dos, tres!"

Three crew members pulled the rope entwined to the engine and after two attempts, the engine roared. The ramp was withdrawn and the *timonil* steered the boat toward the sea while another crew member pushed the boat around with a long bamboo pole. The engine hummed along with the chatter of passengers, steady like a heartbeat while the boat navigated the narrow passage between the islets that were perfect cover for the boats during storms. I watched the outrigger wistfully as it kissed the sea and created bubbles as we surged toward the open seas. Two crew members sit on either side of the outrigger with their sun-kissed back against the noonday sun.

Homecomings always bring a kaleidoscope of emotions; the orgy of faces, fresh and old mixed with a flurry of memories. Most of the time, I could not match the names and the faces anymore so I just smiled and made simple replies when somebody talked to me. In each homecoming, I could see older faces of the people I grew up with while some have passed on. "They've gone ahead" people say, while we soldier on because death is certain. I tried to recall our last conversation on the dock during my last homecoming a few years ago. I was with my older brother and sister with their families, the first time in more than ten years since their last visit.

"Do you still live in Las Pinas?"

"No. I have moved to Pasig". I recognize the old woman at my back as the mother of Helen who was my brother's neighbor in Las Pinas.

"I bet you are earning big now." She teased me.

"Just enough." I said timidly. I got my pocket mirror to check if there was dust on my face and pretended to be busy.

The summer sea was as calm as a well-oiled head, smooth and not a single strand out of place. A sea gull gilded and dipped on the water and flew towards the rocky cliffs of the nearby islet. We were now at the point where the opposite currents meet, where whirlpools developed especially during typhoons. Not a few boats have capsized in this part that has claimed several lives. Locals believe that this part was where the *kataw* lived who fiercely guarded the place from destructive fishing. It was her getting angry in the form of the whirlpool, people claimed. Sometime, she fancied a fisherman and gave him plenty of harvest. Other times, she took one to the depths of the sea and was never seen again, their sea-bound spirits became *santelmo*. Thankfully, we only encountered rolling waves in this part so we didn't mind. I imagined her gliding playfully with the waves along with the dolphins or a returning sea turtle trying to find her way back to her birthplace to lay her eggs.

I remembered Dada Tersing whose house was adjacent to our farm house across the rice field. During farming season, my sisters and I would sleep with her to hear stories about fairies, giants, elves and mermaids. I haven't heard from her since I left for Tacloban after my high school graduation. I hoped she was still alive so I can hear the stories of my childhood.

The boat was now approaching Timontimon point where the lighthouse stood mightily on top of a rocky cliff guiding the ships on moonless nights. I felt that the lighthouse beaconed me after a long absence. I was glad that I was wearing my shades so the other passengers did not see the pooling of tears in my eyes. I took my camera and took as many pictures of the lighthouse from different angles as the motorboat speeded along. I averted my gaze to the white shoreline and the swaying coconut trees as if waving and welcoming me in their bosom once again.

Before I knew it, our motorboat was approaching Looc Bay. I could now see the faces of the people at the shore waiting for us to dock. The engine man dropped the anchor a few meters before we moored. Immediately, children clung to the outriggers as the boat slowed down to look at the passengers inside. I was once like them waiting for my older siblings to go home every single fiesta. Each year, I was disappointed.

I got up along with the other passengers, clutched my hand bag and got ready to disembark. The same boy grabbed my arm to steady myself on the ramp until I came down from the boat. I slid my tired feet on the water, feeling the sensation of sand slipping through my toes while inhaling the salty smell of the sea.

"I will bring your luggage to your house".

"You know my house?"

"Of course! Everybody knows your house".

Well, everybody knew everyone in the village. As a child, I knew all the houses of my friends inside and out. We took turns in playing at each other's houses while our parents were away on the fields so we knew all the rooms inside. Most houses in our village had one big room for the parents and a smaller one for the young women. The other children sleep in a common room in palm mats rolled up during the day. The pillows were stacked in one place in the big room while the clothes were put on empty milk boxes. Only the more affluent families had clothes cabinets.

Tarpaulins courtesy of the Hermana Mayor welcomed the visitors at the wharf. The festive mood was palpable in the air with bannerettes laced together on the streets. I passed by the plaza where people cheered for the competing basketball teams. From there, I could see the faint smoke rising from our kitchen and I knew how busy the household was.

"I'm home!"

"Uy! Your Uncle is here!" Nanay told my young niece who eyed me suspiciously as she hid behind Nanay's skirt.

Nanay and Tatay have grown older since my last visit. Tatay's face broke into a wide grin as he emerged from the kitchen and I reached out for his hand.

"How's the plane ride from Manila? I bet you are now used to riding airplanes", said Nanay.

"If you want, I can book you for a plane ride to Manila by July. You can have a vacation for a month with Tatay".

"Isn't it scary?"

"No. You will only sit down in the plane. But you can look out the window"

"I'm afraid of heights. I may get sick and throw up in the plane. That would be embarrassing."

"It will only take an hour. Before you know it, the plane has landed".

Tatay did not say a word but I saw in his eyes that he was excited for his first plane ride. He has not visited Manila for a long time. The last time was when I was in grade school when he and Nanay visited my older siblings in Manila. I was crying most nights because I missed Nanay terribly. They were away for about two weeks but it felt like a very long time for me. I would ask Elsa when Nanay was coming back but I kept forgetting and expected them to be home when I woke up the following day. Tata Bala looked after us while our parents were away.

I had been working in Manila for ten years now after I left Tacloban for good. I would have wanted to live in Tacloban longer but finally decided to leave for Manila to bring my older siblings home. Our parents have been longing to see them and meet their grandchildren. Our first homecoming happened in my second year in Manila which became a family reunion of sorts. Nanay and Tatay were overjoyed to see their grandchildren, some of whom were not yet born during their last visit. Since then, my two older siblings have relocated back to the island after they got married to one of our *kababayan*. Mana Cion met her husband in a dance in Marikina while Mano Jun returned for good after he had an accident that left him hard of hearing in one ear. It was the last time that Nanay went to Manila to take care of him after he left college more than twenty years before. My first memory of him was when I went to Manila in my junior year in college. I visited him in Las Pinas during one of our performance breaks. It was awkward because I barely knew him and we both didn't know where to start to catch up. We exchanged a few sentences, him asking how our parents were and me telling him that they were okay. The next time I saw him was already in Capul, three years after our first meeting when I was home for the Christmas holiday. I had been working then and we had a memorable New Year celebration at home with seven of us siblings and their children. I remember us talking about how nice it would be if all of us were home on one occasion so when I resigned from my teaching post at the Visayas State University, I decided to apply for a job in Manila and promised my parents to bring my siblings home before our parents became too old.

My Capul-based siblings were at home in anticipation of my homecoming and to help in the preparation for the fiesta. Mano Jun remarried and had a small house near the dock.

After a while, the teenage boy brought in my other luggage and I handed him some tokens. In the kitchen, our helpers were busy cooking. The pig had been butchered. They've set up a makeshift fireplace at the back where a big cauldron of piping hot water for scalding the pig was boiling. I watched the smoke on the thatched roof of our neighbors. Every kitchen was busy.

Nanay insisted on serving me *dinuguan* and rice even if I told her that I had eaten my lunch in Matnog. I instantly salivated after eying the tub of pickled papaya sitting at the dining table.

Meanwhile, my nephews and nieces helped themselves to my *pasalubong*. Everyone had their names on the loot; shirts, dresses, perfumes, bags, slippers and chocolates for both the little ones and the grownups. Everyone was brimming with joy as they got their share. I got Tatay a new transistor radio with extra batteries while Nanay got a new dress for the fiesta.

The water container in the newly refurbished comfort room was filled to the brim. The water was cool in the earthen jar that was once owned by Tata Bala, a souvenir from the old family house in the *poblacion*.

I woke up at dusk feeling disoriented from my extended siesta. It took a few moments before I realized where I was and I smiled at the thought of knowing where I was. From my room, I could hear the happy chatter of Nanay and the helpers and I could smell the wilted banana leaves that they used in wrapping the *suman*. I headed to the wharf to check messages on my cellular phone. The messages were mostly from my co-workers asking if I had arrived home safely to which I replied one after the other.

After a few minutes, the horizon changed from blazing orange to a calmer hue of tangerine and finally, the sun gave way to the glimmer of distant stars and before long they filled the luminescent skies. When I felt alone in a foreign land, I gazed up at the stars from my window, reminding myself that they were the same stars that I looked up to at home. I'd imagine Nanay telling my nephews and nieces about the same constellation that she told us when we were young. Even now, I still wish on falling stars hoping that they send good things to Nanay while I am away.

The balmy weather was compensated by the soft breeze coming from the north as I gazed at the stars – looking for star patterns in the sky. There was the dipper, the archer, the lover's necklace and some others I could not remember. Nanay used to point them to us from the window of our farm house after taking our supper. More galaxies came out as the evening wore on and more people gathered at the sea shore either to look for better phone signals or simply to enjoy the summer breeze. The docked motorboats looked like sentinels of the bay while some crew members started loading copra and beer bottles for the early morning trip to Matnog. More *balikbayans* were expected to arrive in the morning as the yearly exodus began.

Chapter 2: Fiesta!

It was the day before the fiesta and the summer of my ninth birthday. I woke up at 5:30 in the morning and immediately grabbed the containers to fetch water from the communal well about two hundred fifty meters from our house. They were actually soy sauce bottles from a few fiestas ago. I had to fill all the water jars to the brim so I had to return three more times with two containers each. The communal well was the only source of drinking water in the village and it was located at the foot of the hill. It was a natural spring where a century old tree stood on. The men dug the area around it and cemented the edges to gather the water and so it would not spill over. The open well in our back yard was for washing and bathing only because it tasted a bit salty in the summer with the sea water seeping in.

People say that the well was guarded by *engkantos* so we have to be careful not to disturb them but the place was already full of villagers that early. My friend Michael was also on his way to the well. He had two half-gallon containers because he was shorter than me.

"Let us hurry, people are already lining their containers this early." Michael walked ahead. We met Mano Lando carrying a big water can on his shoulders.

"The water level is already low. Hurry up!" Mano Lando coaxed us. We were almost running now.

The houses along the way were already busy. We could hear the shrieks of the hapless pigs being slaughtered. There was excitement in the air with the voices of men telling silly jokes loudly while butchering the pig. Mano Puti was cleaning the pig's entrails in the creek, soaking them in young banana leaves to get rid of their smell. My mouth water on the thought of Nanay's *dinuguan* with green chilies and freshly cracked black pepper. When we reached the well, a few people had lined up their containers and we were afraid that we would scratch more sand than water once our time came.

During summers, the water level of the well goes so low so some villagers looked for other sources farther up the river or in the other villages uphill. Sometimes, I had to go up to Baquiw because even the artesian wells would only vomit sandy water so its mouth was fitted with an old stocking to filter the water.

That afternoon, I re-filled the jars so we have enough until the day of the fiesta. It would be a disgrace if one runs out of drinking water on fiesta.

The village only came to life on the days leading to the fiesta. Elsa and Daria replaced the curtains and covered the walls with wall paper to make them look presentable. I was assigned to wax and scrub the floor with coconut husks again and again until they shine. Afterwards, we washed the plates, glasses, spoons and forks that we borrowed from Dada Felising and dried them on the bamboo table that Tatay constructed beside the open well. They have initials engraved on them so we can identify and return them after the fiesta. Tatay and Dong designed the bamboo fence facing the street like multiple pyramids so they looked nice. The benches at the front yard were also mended. Days before the fiesta, the fire woods were stacked in the backyard and I made sure the surroundings were free from garbage that I burned in the pit. The house looked divine.

At the back, Dong and Mano Boyet replaced the tattered walls and roof of the toilet with woven coconut fronds. Next to it was a small shed that functioned as the extension of our kitchen where most of the food preparations were done like peeling and cutting the vegetables, pounding the garlic, slicing the onions, chilies and ginger and of course the meat. Children were not allowed inside the house while the mayhem was happening so after my chores, I swam in the ocean with the other children until we toasted in the sun.

After breakfast, Dong, Daria and I harvested young coconut for the buko salad and *nilanggang*. The one for the *nilanggang* should be a little bit older than that used for the salad.

Our farm house was long gone after it was toppled down by Typhoon Dinang in 1981 when our youngest Amira was born but the old cotton tree still stood proud in its place, scattering spools of cotton from its cracked overripe fruits as the wind blew. We did not build another house in the same spot again as advised by the shaman so we built a new house, a smaller one in the eastern part of the property. By this time we have settled in the village although we stayed in the farm during farming seasons. According to the shaman, the old house stood on the way of all traffic and the elementals took fancy of the people inside. Nanay felt that the elemental spirits became more aggressive whenever she was pregnant. So when I was of school age, we reside permanently in the village although my parents still went to the farm everyday but would return home to the village by dusk. We had a temporary hut in another part of the property that also served as a smoking shed for copra. This was where my parents cooked their lunch and rested during the hotter hours when the new house was also destroyed by the succeeding typhoons.

Near the old house was a macopa tree that has withstood the annual typhoons although a big branch broke during the last one. They were actually twin trees standing side by side with their respective branches extending opposite each other so that they looked like a single tree from afar. This tree was planted by Tata Bala when my eldest uncle was born. For each child, he planted at least one fruit tree including those that did not make it to adulthood so that the property was fenced by the row of langka, santol, guyabano and mangoes along with bananas and plantains of different variety. Every October, the macopa bursts with pink flowers and when the petals fall, they cover the ground like a red carpet. The bell-shaped fruits ripen in December turning from white to pink and finally into deep crimson. They were sweet-sour when ripe. Sometimes, they bloom off-season so I checked the low branches for random fruits but there was none. Instead, I spotted a plump ripe papaya from what was left of those made into *achara*.

Dong checked the perfect young coconut from tree to tree. He could tell by the sound of the shell as he knocked on them. The flesh has to be firm but soft and should not be mushy as well. Dong opened a couple of coconuts and we drank its juice, cool and sweet in the morning. While Dong was looking for the perfect coconut, Daria and I plucked banana leaves as wrapper for the *nilanggang*.

Elsa and Mano Boyet were pounding rice when we arrived. Our cousin Nena helped them by sifting the powdered rice, making sure that they were fine. I wilted the banana leaves over an open fire and cut them into squares. Nanay mixed the powdered rice with the grated young coconut, sugar and coconut water. Then we formed the banana leaves into cones, poured the mixture in it and steamed. After an hour, I could smell its sweet aroma wafting from the kitchen. You can tell that it was done when the banana leaves had completely wilted, Nanay opened a couple and we shared the goodness of *nilanggang*.

At dusk Tatay lit the petromax. He installed the gauze burner carefully which he moistened in alcohol fluid, pumped kerosene into the tank and adjusted the valve until the light was steady. One has to be careful because the gauze burner can easily break. 'Tis the only time that the house was lighted this bright except on occasions when Tatay and my brothers went night fishing. Tatay used to fish when he was younger but he got pulmonary tuberculosis from being exposed to the elements so he had to stop and focus on farming. We hung the petromax between the dining room and the living room to maximize the light. In the kitchen and at the shed, we installed electric light bulbs that we rented from the sound system so that we had light all night long. The house looked different with the bright lights. Outside, you can see the holes in the thatched walls and roof that needed to be mended before the onslaught of the rainy season.

At the plaza, the sound system had been set-up. The tables and chairs from the elementary school were brought in including the pews from the chapel; the chairs and pews were installed around the basketball court where the ladies will sit. The colorful lights and the disco ball were installed at the center that made the children excited. When the music started playing, they danced like crazy because by eight o'clock in the evening, only the adults who bought tickets were allowed to dance. The girls wore their best dresses and the boys approached those they liked to dance with.

Around the plaza and on the streets, vendors sold haluhalo, fruits, shirts, dresses, slippers, toys of different kinds and kitchen utensils.

Our cousin Luz put up her store in front of our house where she sold liquor, soft drinks, candies and a variety of food items. She had been a regular every fiesta since I remembered. Among those sold during the fiesta, my favorite was cotton candy. I was mesmerized by it spinning in the wheel and then expertly scooped by the vendor with a bamboo stick. I also bought myself a new pair of slippers from the sales of my *gulaman*. When I slept that night, I hid my new slippers near my bed, afraid that they would be stolen.

By dinnertime, the house was full of relatives so we served food in several batches. We served vegetables, *dinuguan* and *pancit bihon*. The special dishes were reserved on the actual day of the fiesta. Besides, we did not have so much.

At the plaza, the sound system blares non-stop chacha music while children swirl and go about enthralled by the colorful and dizzying disco lights until they are escorted out of the dancing area.

"Good evening everyone. Welcome and happy fiesta to us all. I am enticing everyone, especially the ladies, to start occupying the seats so we can start our celebration tonight." It was Mana Felina, the barangay secretary inviting everyone to the dance. Tickets were sold at P5.00 each and the adult men received a ribbon pinned to their chest as proof so they could enter or exit the plaza with ease.

The barangay officials and teachers manned the ticket booth and the presidential table, where the mayor and other special guests were seated. Mrs. Bandal, my Grade One teacher was the emcee for the night so she took over the microphone from Baba Amboy, the Barangay Captain. Young ladies started arriving at the plaza. They smell of cologne and talc, their lips red and their cheeks blushed as they pass by our house wearing their Sunday dress. Their heels clicked on concrete.

Outside the dancing hall, the village people converged to see who got the best moves. The onlookers pitied the girl who was not asked by anyone to dance. Old women were reduced to being spectators gawking by the concrete fence. They had their time when they were younger.

"That girl is warming her seat so much she might burn them." Mana Lilia remarked with a smirk, pointing to the girl seated near the light post.

"That girl will marry early." Mana Maring pointed to the most sought after girl with a body hugging dress. I tried to peek inside the dancing hall but the thick wall of people pushed me back. Then the music stopped to signal the *kuracha*.

The vesper day dance was the most sought after, where politicians flashed their money and the *balikbayans* showed off their new-found status: fairer skin, flamboyant dresses, shiny and stylish shoes and money to spare. The first pair was the town mayor and the *hermana* mayor. They sashayed, swayed their hands and hips, and threw paper bills to the wind to the delight of the people and the organizers had to double time in picking the bills. The next pair was the vice mayor and the young wife of a retired US Marine who did not want to be upstaged. The white husband had been oriented about the local custom and would throw money at every opportunity. The third pair was the Kapitan and the School principal who were more modest but were also generous in giving the spectacle that the people love. Three *kuratsa* numbers were done every so often because the dance was mainly a fundraising event for the church and other projects of the barangay. The rich guests especially those coming from Manila displayed their new-found status by showering paper bills every opportune time that the organizers had to put a bigger basket for the *gala*.

Years later when I was in high school and college, I would be tasked to host the dances which I found tiring because I had to announce the exact titles and ranks of each dancer, even those of former barangay councilor, their ranks in government service or those in the military service. I got called out several times to indicate the correct titles of the guests so I directed them to the secretariat.

Outside the plaza, a commotion ensued and momentarily stopped the dance. Mano Filo had been stabbed. People ran in different directions. The music stopped. Baba Amboy took the microphone pleading with the people to respect Nuestra Senora de Salvacion and for the police to take charge. Mano Edgar, the assailant was caught red handed. He was drunk and could not run any farther. His relatives wanted to hide him but they were warned that they will be included in the complaint.

"It was a long-standing feud between two families". Baba Mario, a police officer reported when he asked for drinking water. "This time, Filo died due to stab wounds in the chest and stomach. I think his vital organs were hit." Baba Mario shook his head.

"What was the cause of the feud? Nanay asked.

"Remember Baldo who was stabbed during the fiesta in Sawang? Clearly, Edgar is seeking vengeance." Baba Mario added.

Nanay forbade us to go out again. Baba Amboy was on the microphone once again and appealed to everyone to respect the celebration. Baba Mario took his place at the main entrance to the plaza. Every now and then, he would escort an obviously drunk man out. One drunken man sat at the bench on our front porch so the other people left and looked for other places to sit. He was still snoring when the church bells toll the following morning, his shirt stained with his own vomit.

The dance resumed like no one just died. It lasted until the morning. The money collected from the *gala* amounted to almost fifty thousand pesos. There was no available space to sleep so I snuck under the bamboo bed. The petromax had run out of gas and only the electric bulbs at the back were on.

I barely slept when the bells started ringing that signaled the start of the high mass. The early guests were served coffee and nilanggang for breakfast. The house was in a whirlwind of activities: my small cousins taking their time bathing in the open well flooding the backyard, Nanay and my sisters doing last minute cooking and washing plates and glasses used the night before. I slipped on my best shirt and changed my shorts with the one that I bought with the remainder of my earnings from selling *gulaman* and the ripe jackfruit that I personally carried on my back from Baquiw, the spikes bore a mark on my shoulders until the following morning.

People started trooping to the chapel with their best clothes, the women with their jewels and make up and the men with their well-coiffed hair fragrant with pomade. The young men and women sported the latest fashion in Manila and spoke Tagalog.

The pews were returned and the sound system had been set-up outside the chapel so people could listen to the mass. People fan themselves under the shade of coconut trees or under the awning of houses near the chapel. My sisters and cousins brought out some chairs outside the house where we sat.

The procession was now returning to the chapel headed by Padre Dulay and the altar boys. The brass band played the hymn of De Salvacion, followed by the *estandarte* held by Mana Idad, the current Hermana Mayor. Mana Quilin and the other old ladies march beside the *karo* which was heavily decorated with ferns and paper roses pushed by the lay ministers on four sides. Nanay and the old women who serve the church were behind the *karo* followed by the other parishioners.

The mass took two hours so it was almost lunchtime when it was finished. We rushed inside to prepare the table so our guests could eat. Although we didn't have much, there was never a time that we ran out of food. Guests usually eat a bit in one house then proceed to other houses. Only our closest friends and relatives stay to have a few drinks while exchanging pleasantries, updates about each other's lives: who has married, who has graduated, who has given birth, or who has gone ahead.

After doing the dishes, Michael and I walked to Parola under the scorching heat of the sun. Other young people were walking too, some of them in pairs to enjoy the breeze under the big talisay tree or on the beach. The passenger motorcycles were also carrying passengers to and from the lighthouse non-stop. Some dared to climb the tower but I could not bring myself to do it again after Nanay brought me up just one month before. The Parola was home to her cousins during school break because Tata Bala's sister was married to the *parolista*.

Chapter 3: Son of the Soil

"Alex, wake up! You have to help your sisters in sorting the seedlings"

Nanay gently rocked my shoulders. I half-opened my eyes and struggled to get up stretching my arms. Nanay was already up and about the house, folding the blankets and rolling up the *pandan* mats in the corner of the common room. Nanay wove the mats herself during the lull months of the farming season. The pillows were also stacked in one corner, on top of the milk cartons where we put our everyday clothes. The clothes were not folded properly and some had tumbled over when someone was looking for something to wear. The more decent clothes that we wear on Sundays and on special occasions were kept in a wooden box scented with camphor balls. I only had one shirt in that wooden box, a light blue shirt that Nanay bought during the last town fiesta that I wore on my recognition day where I got third honors in second grade.

In the living room, the rice seedlings were scattered on a *buri* mat with the kerosene lamp at the center. Elsa and Daria were carefully untangling the balls of sprouted rice grains so that they can be scattered easily on the seedbed. The sprouted seedlings were about a week old and kept in the shade.

After relieving myself in the bathroom, I joined my sisters quietly until we finished two sacks that Dong carried to the rice field in Baquiw. The seeds have to be scattered early, before the birds awake.

Tatay has left ahead to prepare the field so after eating my breakfast of coconut rice and dried fish, grilled in the embers of the open hearth, I carried the basket containing Tatay's breakfast. Dong and Mano Boyet took one sack each and followed shortly after Tatay.

The cold morning dew tickled my bare feet as we trekked the three kilometer mountain trail. I brushed the undergrowth as we passed along the corn fields of Mano Lope on the slope of the hill. Mung beans were planted alternate the rows while cassava were planted on the edge of the clearing. On the roadside I picked *asin-asin* flowers and sucked their nectar. They tasted sweeter in the morning.

A gray crow stirs in the bush and flies to the nearby guava tree. It flapped its ruffled dark brown feathers as it hurriedly flew again to the nearby bush. They say that it was bad luck to encounter the bird this early in the morning so we shooed him away. A hornbill flew over us and settled at the branch of a pili nut on the adjacent farm of Baba Erling.

The sun was peeking from the mountaintops as we started descending to the farm house on the edge of the rice fields. The terraced rice fields, carved from the surrounding hills by our great grandfathers, looked serene in the early morning sun. The mist started to lift off the hills and the clearing like smoke from the thatched roof of the few houses scattered along the hills. The adjoining farms were owned by relatives who inherited them also from their grandfathers. The fields were now farmed by different cousins taking turns every season. These were the same people that we worked with every season, our lives intertwined by monsoon rains or droughts that sometimes plague this little community.

The newly ploughed field smelled of burnt grass and carabao dung. The animal patiently carried the yoke slung on its neck, the blade tearing up the soil, opening new wounds on the ground as it burrows. Ground worms wriggle as they hang from the newly ploughed soil. I stopped for a while watching Tatay's thin frame as he commandeered the animal on the field; his leathery complexion made darker by the seasons. His right hand gripped the saddle tightly that he also used to direct the carabao around the field, his left hand on the handle of the plough, pulling and loosening the rope to signal the animal.

"Ho! Ho! Ho!" Tatay halted the carabao at the end of the paddy. He moved the plough to the opposite direction and pulled the rope. "Tsk! Tsk! Tsk!" he directed the poor animal that was grazing on the remaining grass on the dike. Onward they ploughed the field, master and subject.

The seedlings have been scattered on the newly prepared seedbed. The seedlings sat on the fresh mud like soft cotton turned upside down. We will have to wait for two to three weeks before they can be transplanted. In the meantime, the paddies will be ploughed and irrigated and the dikes mended.

Dong was fixing the dikes on the other side of the field. His taut muscles flexed as he drove the pickaxe up and down to carve the dike. His sweat runs down his exposed torso from his cut-off shirt. He was four years older than me. Dong has taken over the responsibility of helping Tatay in the farm, a bigger percentage of which were owned by our cousins from my mother's side. Only the small portion that Nanay inherited from Tata Bala was ours so we only took home a portion of the harvest. To compensate for it, Tatay was sharecropping with his cousins in different farms so we had enough rice to last the next harvest. After the field in Baquiw, Tatay and my brothers will do the fields in Malpal, and then Kalurusan that Tatay also shared with Baba Cesar and lastly in Ilawod so we need to finish before the monsoons flood the dikes and submerge the saplings.

Mano Boyet cleared the tall grasses on the other part of the paddy. He seemed not happy with his task as he stops often, checking his splintered hands and looking desolate. He looked ill-fitted for farm work with his carefully coiffed hair and good-looking features. He got his good looks from Tata Iling, our paternal grandfather who had Spanish blood.

A few minutes later, Tatay, Mano Boyet and Dong momentarily halted their tasks and took their breakfast on the shed after washing their soiled hands at the irrigation canal. I prepared banana leaves from where they will eat their breakfast, still warm from the boxes. They ate in silence.

"Tie a rope around the seedbed to scare the birds before you retire for the morning and put coconut fronds around it."

Without looking at Tatay, Dong took his bolo and looked for dried coconut fronds and did as he was instructed. Tatay resumed ploughing while I and my sisters went with Nanay to the vegetable patch on the foot of the hill while Mano Boyet got his bolo and went to the back of the shed, grabbed the unfinished ukulele that he started to carve a few days ago from the trunk of the jackfruit tree and continued carving, polishing the wood and shaping the body. Mano Boyet was in high school and the only reason why he passed his subjects was because he sang in school programs as requested by his teachers. Otherwise, he would have failed in every single subject because he didn't attend his classes according to Baba Maco who was one of his teachers. The girls admire his singing talent as well as his rugged good looks and he used his charm to get his way with his female teachers.

The eggplant seedlings that we transplanted a week ago have started to get sturdier and their leaves greener. I removed the fern leaves that we used to cover the seedlings to shield them from too much heat or too much rain as they will not propagate too well. The okra planted alternately with the eggplants had germinated too. I carefully trudged on the furrows so as not to step on the plants.

Armed with flat-tipped blunt bolos, we weeded out the parasites and water the plants from the nearby brook. We also fenced the patch with dried bamboo branches to deter the wandering animals from burrowing on the plants.

"Oh Lord most high, make this earth generous once again as we plant these seeds."

"Oh ancestors of old, who once tilled this land, I summon you to look after us as we till this land once more. Guard them from pests and insects and help us to have a bountiful harvest."

"Oh spirits of the land, of the trees, the brooks and the wind, help us guard this land from pests and birds."

"Oh San Isidro Labrador, guide us and bless us with a bountiful harvest."

Eyes closed, Mana Babing stood on the edge of the seedbed, arms folded on her breast. It was the first day of the transplanting season and the rice seedlings were ready. The saplings swayed with the gentle blowing of the wind like blue-green waves dancing to every word of the incantations. Mana Babing touched the succulent plants with her outstretched hands while murmuring the incantations. Then she pulled a handful of sapling as she concluded her prayers and pleadings and put them on the dike.

It was officially the start of the new planting season.

Dong showed me how to uproot the saplings properly. The plants were tender and they easily broke when not handled properly.

"Grab the rice saplings at the base with both of your hands then pull them all together. Quickly remove the mud from the roots with your right hand." I did as he did and learned quickly. I watched Nanay, Elsa and Daria pulling the saplings like how Dong taught me and copied them as well.

Bent from waist down, my siblings uprooted the saplings effortlessly and tied each handful with the tender blades of the saplings. My hips ache so I looked for coconut husks to sit on. When we had enough seedlings to plant, Nanay and my older sisters started transplanting the saplings in the freshly made paddies. Being short, I could not move easily in the mud so I was tasked to distribute the saplings for the planters which I did while walking in the still soft dikes.

The swarm of river shrimps in the irrigation canal caught my attention so when I was done with my tasks, I got an old mosquito net and installed it across the mouth of the canal and tried driving the little creatures to the net. Before lunchtime, I was able to gather a handful which we cooked together with some *camote* tops.

The other paddies in Baquiw to Bel-at were also being planted. These were the same families working on this side every farming season. Some of them live nearby so they go home for lunch. Others came from other villages and went home before dusk. Although the task was taxing, no one was complaining about it. The farmers exchanged happy chatter every now and then, talking about their daily chores and domestic concerns; their bodies bent from the waist down, moving in the same rhythm, their backs against the sun. Thankfully, the sun dimmed with the passing of the large group of cumulus clouds and threatened to rain, giving a much-needed respite although it was not until after lunch that it poured while we were resting. The rain spattered on the roof of the shed then abruptly stopped an hour later, cooling the fields and turning the slopes more slippery than when we ascended in the morning.

The newly transplanted rice looked like pastel paintings on a still canvass with tadpoles and river shrimps creating tiny bubbles on the surface. The saplings were planted slanted on the mud. In a week's time, they will straighten up, darker in color and sturdier. The water from the irrigation canal should flow continuously while they grow.

By lunchtime, we finished planting two big paddies. Tatay led the carabao in the guava bush near the brook while Nanay, Dong, Daria and I headed to the nearby marsh. Elsa, who had weak lungs, rested earlier than us and was tasked to cook rice while Tatay gathered some coconuts and fire wood.

We washed off the dried soil that caked in our clothes and thighs in the irrigation canal and headed off to the marsh near Bel-at and caught some crabs and gather snails and mollusks in the tide pools. Mud crabs and snails were aplenty during the planting season.

"Pick a handful of soft mud before you insert it in the hole so you will not get bitten by the crab." Dong instructed me as I inspected the first hole I saw in the mangroves. "The moment you touch the crab, push it against the soil and grab it at the back of its claws."

Dong cautioned me to be careful in choosing a hole, lest I could catch snakes.

"Look for the finger marks at the mouth of the hole before inserting your hands. Other holes are not that of crabs. " Dong added while showing me potential holes among several near the puddle among the roots of the mangroves. "Oftentimes, the hole leads to a labyrinth of other shallow holes. Look for the downward hole because that is where they hide during the day". I do the same as he instructed but I forgot all of it when I got bitten by the first crab that I cornered on the hole. Dong rushed to my rescue.

I contented myself in gathering snails, shells and mollusks on the tide pools. The horn snails can be easily spotted in the mounds because they leave a line as they move. *Dalu-dalo* on the other hand cling to the roots of the mangroves, exposed by the low tide.

Elsa has gathered sweetpotato tops while Mano Boyet has grated the coconut when we arrived with a basket full of crabs and another basket of *sabiran* and *daludalo*. We had a hearty lunch, eating with our hands while listening to the transistor radio. The announcer warned of more rains with the coming of the northwest monsoon in August. Mano Boyet tested the new strings in his ukulele and hummed a song. His soft singing made us all drowsy and fell asleep and the rhythm of the spattering rain on the roof sent us through dreamland.

The siesta energized all of us. The soft breeze from the east blew and it was our cue to resume. The rain had completely stopped. We grabbed our long sleeve shirts and put on our *buri* hats and headed to the rice fields again.

Dong gathered some coconut fronds and erected them on his work station as a shield against the sun so he can work in the seedbed. Mano Boyet joined Nanay and my sisters in transplanting so we finished all the paddies by sundown.

The hornbill took its flight to the marsh from the forest announcing the end of the working day with a soft but hoarse screech. It was five thirty. The planters finished transplanting the saplings in their hands and stretched out their backs and hips before heading to the irrigation canal to wash off the caked mud and refreshed before heading home.

Tatay got more coconuts to be brought home. I joined Nanay and my sisters in picking winged beans hanging among the bushes at the edge of the clearing. Mano Boyet gathered firewood while Dong carried the water container on his shoulders and headed the pack. We retraced our steps in the footpath going down the village before it became too dark.

On the roadside, ripe guavas were inviting on low branches so I ran ahead of Nanay and my sisters so I would not fall too far back. It was also a season of *saging-saging* and *dulce kurumbot* so I had my pockets bursting to the seams.

As we passed by the house of Dada Juling, she invited us in.

"Uy! Stay for a while. We have boiled young corn. It is sweet and soft." Dada Juling invited us inside the house but we stopped at the front yard where she brought benches and the steaming boiled young corn.

"Here." My cousin Belen offered.

I greedily munched on the young corn and drank spring water from an empty Caltex can. The elders passed around a glass of coconut wine, to relax the tired muscles, they say.

The foxfires were bright on the dead woods by the foot path when we started our final descent to the village, ever careful not to step on loose stones as we navigated the slippery downhill slopes. I picked some foxfires and put them on my palms, fascinated with their luminescent glow. When we got home, I put them on the bedside table. They illuminated brighter in the dark when the kerosene lamp dried up and was finally extinguished.

The following morning, a light drizzle preceded our ascent to the hills so I pulled over my *buri* hat. The soft mud slipped on my toes as I navigated the slippery earth and I tightened my grip on the basket of breakfast for Tatay and my brothers. On the roadside were small streams of rain water cascading to the brook that bordered the properties of different families. I crossed the brook stepping on the boulders that functioned as a natural bridge to the other side. I got tempted to catch the shrimp fries that gathered in the pool but I was already lagging behind Nanay and my sisters. In a few months, the shrimps and eels will be big enough to harvest. Dong will set out bamboo traps for the mud crabs along the brooks and an old net for the shrimps that Nanay will cook with young coconut meat, their fats staining the stew with natural orange color.

The view on top of the hill was breath-taking. I marveled at the eastern and western seas and inhaled as much air before descending to the valley where our farm house was. I trailed behind Nanay and my sisters as we brushed aside the wet grass and foliage that felt cold on our thighs.

Nanay blew the hot ash of the heart and hung the pot of fish stew on a hook beneath the glowing coal to prevent the stray cats from opening the lid. I scooped spring water from the earthen jar with a coconut shell and put on my straw hat before going out.

We finished transplanting the remaining rice seedlings before sundown. At dusk, we returned to the village with a basket of sweet potato that we harvested quickly at the nearby *kaingin*. Dong checked his *padlong* and got some mud crabs that was perfect for *kinagang*. He installed the bamboo traps on the holes in the dikes with leaves as bait. When the crab got out of their holes in the evening to look for food, they got trapped inside the *padlong*.

The crickets murmured on the bushes and the foxfires glowed on the roadside as we descended on the slippery hills of Banakod. We passed by Baba Julio tying firewood and getting ready to go home. Nanay and Baba Julio exchanged short pleasantries as we passed along.

We retrieved our water containers hidden in the bush and filled them at the artesian well and put on our worn-out slippers, washed our feet as we approached the village.

Transplanting was done before the weekend so we cleared a fresh *kaingin* afterwards. The area planted with sweet potato yielded less and less after a few harvests. Tatay and Dong cleared the western part of the farm house, near the creek while Mano Boyet reluctantly joined them, choosing a spot with lower undergrowth to clear. The other farmers nearby helped us in clearing the site. Nanay prepared fish stew and rice for everybody. The bushes were overgrown where there was once cassava and corn a few seasons back. The soil has to replenish its nutrients naturally and should be left unattended for some time while another part of the land will be cleared and planted. On the periphery of the clearing were bananas of different varieties. On their roots, mushrooms sprung during thunderstorms which we gathered and cooked wrapped in banana leaf and roasted in hot embers.

By sundown, we cleared half a hectare of kaingin. The farmers shared two gallons of coconut wine with the leftover fish as *sumsuman*. Loud singing followed. Laughter was heard from the other side of the hill.

There was always so much work to be done in the farm: weeding and watering the seedlings, cultivating the soil and plucking out the worms and pests so that when the buds become flowers and the fruits are ready for picking, the farmer is rewarded of his hard work.

"You will never go hungry if you know how to till the land. The land may not always be generous but when you plant something, it will bear fruit." Nanay said as we picked the young eggplants hanging from their tender buds. She carefully plucked the fruits from the stem, ever careful not to hurt the plant. I followed after her.

"However, you have to take care of your plants so they will thrive. You do not plant and then abandon your farm and expect that they grow by themselves. There are plants that grow best in a particular season and in different soils. You have to cultivate different plants so you can have food in any season". Nanay continued as we picked the string beans hanging from the vines clinging to the bamboo fence.

We tied the eggplants in fives and tens and bundled the string beans to be sold around the village. But I don't need to go around because people flocked around us as soon as we passed by the first houses in the village.

After three full moons, the corn was ready for harvest when their leaves dried up. Some corns produce new branches and bear new fruits that do not reach maturity when the main trunks have dried up. We skewered them on split bamboo and grilled them in an open fire. This was our reward in helping the harvest.

Neighbors helped each other in un-husking the corn kernels. There were no corn mills on the island by this time so Tatay brought them to Bulan Sorsogon where he would stay overnight with some relatives. On his return, he would bring sweetened popped corn in a tin biscuit can. This was the treat that I looked forward to after every corn harvest.

To extend our food supply, Nanay mixed the corn meal and rice to last until the next harvest. She cooked the corn flour with coconut milk and sugar for breakfast or *merienda*. Nanay can also be creative with the corn flour. This recipe I remember from memory is called tabon-tabon.

>Tabon-tabon
>
>Procedure:
>
>Roast the corn flour over low fire
>
>Prepare shredded young coconuts and sugar
>
>Mix the roasted corn flour, sugar, coconut water and shredded young coconut (*lukaron*), mash and form into balls. In a big cauldron,

put a tin plate upside down at the bottom and put water. Boil over low fire for about one hour or until the balls are cooked.

Food was not always scarce in our family because we produced what we eat.

Chapter 4: Lost in the woods

The river snaked through the mangroves and rice fields and emptied into the Looc Bay. The fish ponds along the banks looked like bald patches against the green marshland while the rocky cliffs of Pundang serve as sentinels at the mouth of the river. Along the cliff were wild orchids that bloomed during the summer ready to decorate the front porches of the houses for the fiesta.

The banks as I remember them were pregnant with shells like *bug-atan* that spits water when you step on them. Mollusks were plentiful and we collected them on the roots of the mangroves and on the tide pools. During low tide, the fiddler crabs emerge from their holes and burrow in the sand but they retreat in their holes when they sense movement on the ground. Their colorful claws were not as powerful as the blue crab that we caught with *bubo*, a cylindrical bamboo trap. When I was younger, I caught and tied fiddler crabs with straw like pets. On the other side of the river near the fish ponds, my friends and I gathered mud crabs that hide on the algae during low tide. They had a slightly softer shell and weaker claws so we caught them with our bare hands. Nanay cooked them the following day so they could excrete the mud in their belly.

The mighty river was once home to freshwater crocodiles but the last of their spawn was caught when I was in the third grade. We were forbidden to wade in the waters off Pundang due to the presence of these dangerous animals. Pundang was also believed to be an enchanted place where supernatural occurrences were observed by several villagers. Nobody really owned it but there were a few villagers who dared to make a clearing and planted them with root crops and vegetables but they abandoned them because of unexplained occurrences like when their bolos suddenly disappeared or became mysteriously ill. The mangrove was also home to birds like the hornbill, hawks, eagles and a colony of bats that looked like dangling evil fruits at day time. When we were small, we used to cast stones at them and when they were disturbed, the bats dispersed to every direction with their eerie squeaking sound.

Some fishermen claimed to have witnessed different phenomena on Pundang like seeing a grand palace in place of the cliffs and gigantic ships approaching the mouth of the river at dusk. Mano Enrique swears he heard a loud horn followed by colossal waves that almost made his canoe capsize so he went home without being able to check all his traps. The families living near the river have stories of mystical appearances on Pundang and a few teenagers have been possessed after venturing into the place including my cousin Borge who had hallucinations of unfamiliar people after getting some branches for his school fencing project. He had a fever for several days and his parents thought that they might lose him so they performed *pagbawi* with a shaman. But for me and my friend Levi, Pundang was an excellent fishing ground. We would perch on the branch of the mangrove and lower our fishing pole with a bait of sea worm on the hungry fishes below. On high tides, the water was clear and you could see the hungry *parangan* going crazy over the bait so that when I withdrew the line, I would catch a few of them in one sitting. Sometimes, a stone fish would take the bait. This was difficult because they would go under the rock when you pull the line, it would snap leaving you without a hook. We would swim back to the other side of the bank and go straight to the bridge where other children played. In fact, I taught myself to swim by jumping from the wooden bridge close to the shore because all the children did that. Besides, it would be a disgrace for an island boy to not be able to swim. As a child, I started by wading in the shallows and then later on, I joined the other children diving the deepest part of the river and getting the white stone we threw in the water.

Perhaps, one of the most enduring stories about the mystery of Pundang is that of the new midwife who was from another town. At this time, the Barangay Health Center was constructed on donated land at the bank of the river overlooking Pundang. One afternoon, the new midwife was roused from her siesta because of the pealing of bells. She looked out the window and saw with her own eyes the majestic palace across the river where a gathering was being held. She saw people dressed splendidly like royals, their shimmering clothes blinding her. Afraid of what she saw, she ran barefoot to the village trembling, telling everybody what she saw. She only went back to the clinic to get her things when she was accompanied by some villagers and she refused to look out the window again. Later on, the clinic was transferred to the residential area in the village.

Nights on the island were dark because there was no electricity. It was not advisable to walk at night especially when going home from the farm because one might hit an engkanto. At dusk when we returned to the village, we could smell food being cooked even in places where there were no houses nearby. We just ignore it and hasten our steps so as not to disturb them. People generally believe that engkantos live in big trees or in rocks or on brooks so one has to excuse himself as he passes by.

People believed that the birds and other animals were the pets of engkantos so when someone hit them, they would be inflicted with a mysterious illness. Some people recovered if the engkanto accepted the gifts offered during the *pabawi*, while others died and were believed to be taken into the world of the engkantos. Later on, people claimed that they were seen near the big trees or in creeks or near the big rocks.

One day in the summer of my tenth birthday, a motorboat full of construction materials docked at midday. The boat was from Matnog, Sorsogon so nobody knew the crew or who ordered the materials. Mana Liding, whose house was beside the chapel said that the crew was instructed to put the bags of cement, plywood and steel bars near Pundang which was practically her backyard. Mana Liding was surprised because nobody lived on the spot and no one was constructing a house nearby. She forgot about them and went on with her tasks. When she looked again, the construction materials had disappeared. The villagers believed that someone was building a house in Pundang.

Mano Doming who trapped blue crabs in Pundang claimed that he heard a loud siren of a big boat followed by big waves one day at dusk. His canoe almost capsized so he immediately went home. He also heard other strange sounds at different times of the day so he got accustomed to it. Sometimes, he saw a big house on top of the cliff but it disappeared the next time he looked.

"Whenever I venture to Pundang, I ask permission from whoever is living in the river and the rocks to let me do my work for my family. You know I am sending two of my children to college at this time." Mano Doming said. "I get used to seeing or hearing strange things in Pundang although I have to admit that I get scared sometimes. My hair would stand on end when I encountered them." He added.

One day when I was around nine years old, Nanay asked me and Dong to harvest some cassava that she will make into *muron*. It was mid-morning when Dong and I started our descent to the farm in Baquiw. The sun was gloomy which was perfect because it was not too hot. When we reached the hilly part of Banakod, Dong and I decided to check the guava trees on the side of the foot path. I found some big ripe fruits and I ate some of them while looking for more. I also went down near the creek where I got some more so my pockets were full. Having checked all the trees, I look around where Dong was but I could not see him. I called his name aloud but he did not answer back so I panicked and started crying. Unable to find Dong, I continued on my way to the farm thinking that Dong may have gone ahead while I was picking guavas.

Dong was not in the farm and I did not see any sign that he had harvested cassava. The patch has no fresh spots so I decided to go back but I did not see anyone along the way. When I passed by Banakod again, I looked and called for him thinking he was playing tricks on me. I did not see any trace of him so I ran back to the village.

Dong was waiting at the house when I arrived.

"Where have you been? I've been looking for you!"

"I was picking guava near the creek and then when I looked around you were gone."

"How could that be when I was calling you and looking around for you?"

"I thought that you had left so I proceeded to the farm. But I did not see you there.

"I was there. I harvested cassava and I have returned but I did not meet you along the way."

I can see Dong's worried look. I cried again when I realized that I and Dong were tricked by some engkanto. We were in the same place but we were in the same plane.

Nanay explained that engkantos live in the same space as we do although they are in another dimension. Sometimes, we are able to penetrate their world but that means that other people will not be able to see us. That is why, Dong and I did not see each other even if we were probably in the same place.

Even in our house, there had been incidents when we were looking for something like a ladle that we were using but it was not in its usual place so we looked everywhere. Suddenly, someone returned it, still dripping wet with some soup. Another time, Daria and I were washing clothes in the well at the back of our neighbor's house when the pail and bamboo pole that we used to draw water suddenly disappeared. We looked for it inside the house and even asked the neighbors but they did not see it. Suddenly, somebody dropped it in the same spot that it was placed. Again, still dripping wet.

In cases such as this, we just keep calm and ask for permission to use the space that they may be in.

Chapter 5: Bladed Verses

I fell asleep on the second verse of the song but I hear the entire song in my dreams including the pauses and sighs as Nanay sang *"Basuni Ko sa Dughan"* (roughly translated as Splinter in My Heart) followed by *"Duyan"* (The Hammock) . I never understood what the song meant but I love their melody. I noticed that Nanay has this pensive look when she sings them. I did not notice that they were two different songs until I was doing research in different parts of Samar after my college graduation many years later. These songs were written by Pablo Rebadulla, a Waray poet who was also a lawyer.

I woke up at around three o'clock and crept carefully out of the mat so as not to disturb Nanay and my younger brother Jonas who was sleeping on the other side and joined my friends in the street. We played skip rope using a vine growing along the sea shore. When we got tired skipping, we ran around the village aiming at unsuspecting passersby with our bamboo toy and pellets made from wet paper.

I ran back to the house panting after more than an hour in the streets. Nanay was making cassava balls. I salivated on the sweet coconut filling but I controlled my cravings until the *jambol* was cooked.

Nanay folded in the mashed overripe plantains with the grated cassava. They were the leftovers from yesterday's banana fritters.

"They will make the balls softer. That way, it is good to eat even if it is already stale." Nanay explained.

I helped my sisters shape the grated cassava into balls.

"Prick the center with your thumb and put sweetened coconut in the center." I do as Daria instructed.

Nanay fried them in coconut oil that she herself made. The balls sizzle with oil bubbles as they cook and then float when they are ready. We skewer them by fives in coconut midribs. Nanay separated some for me and I ate them when they cooled down.

Sales were brisk. I returned with fifty pesos and some pre-orders. Even the newly cooked jambol at home were sold out within an hour.

Baba Serafin's visit the following morning was not really conspicuous because he has visited us several times in the past. He was Mano Gilbert's father, Mano Jun's boarding house roommate at the University.

I saw them talking in a hushed voice in the living room. Tatay was pacing the room and shaking his head. I could see the disappointment in his sighs. Then I overheard what they were talking from my place in the kitchen.

"Jun has left the University. But he did not tell anyone before he left. Not even Gilbert." Baba Serafin said tentatively. Tatay and Nanay are devastated.

"What could be his problem? He did not mention anything when he was here during the Christmas vacation." Nanay found a seat on the sack of copra that Tatay was supposed to sell the following day.

"We just sent him money and his provisions until the end of the month." Tatay was becoming irritated.

"Gilbert asked their friends and their classmates but Jun did not mention anything to anyone about his plan. He did not mention any plans to leave. So Gilbert is clueless." Baba Serafin mentioned.

Tatay set for Catarman the next day. He was expected to arrive in two days because the highway was still under construction during this time. He has to look for lodging along the way and board another jeepney to continue the trip to the university town. It was common knowledge that the rebel groups were taking control of some parts of the highway to the university town while the government soldiers had detachments in other parts. Reports say that there was an encounter between the government soldiers and the rebels the previous month so it was extremely risky to travel at night even in groups.

The University of the Eastern Philippines is located in the capital town of Catarman with its surroundings of lush forest cover to the west and the beach to the east. The rebel group was said to be camping in the forested area near the campus and was actively recruiting students as intelligence operatives. I heard on the neighbor's transistor radio that the anti-government sentiments are high during this time due to supposed excesses of the military in cracking down rebels and their sympathizers. Dada Titay said some farmers were suspected of being sympathizers of the rebels. Men and women were brought to the military camps for questioning. She has seen some of them on the clearing near her farm in Tangulon village in San Isidro town. She heard that some were tortured and summarily executed. Others disappeared without a trace while others enlisted with the rebel group altogether.

Dada Titay visited us the previous month and brought us pineapples from her farm, or what was left of her harvest. She suspected that the rebels took some of her fruits and she was grateful that they had the decency to leave some for her. She was thankful though that the rebels only took her fruits and they did not harm her. Dada Titay has been a widow for some time. I did not remember her husband because he died due to heart failure while I was still a toddler. She had three grown-up children, two of whom are now based in Manila, while the youngest, a teenage boy, was the one helping her in the farm.

Electricity was only available in the campus from six to ten in the evening so the students contended with kerosene lamps especially since some boarding houses do not have the connection. The dark nights were the perfect cover for secret meetings and organizing of the sympathizers of the left-wing rebels.

I was too young to understand all of this. Later on when I was of school age, I learned that the students in the University of the Philippines and other schools in Manila were staging rallies to fight for press freedom while the farmers were fighting for land ownership. Rallies and demonstrations in campuses in Manila denouncing the despotic rule were only reported in underground publications and campus papers because only the state media was allowed to operate.

The First Lady wanted only "the good and the beautiful" to be reported in the national media while she and the rest of the first family partied with Hollywood celebrities and international politicians displaying their excessive lifestyle while hundreds of families had little or nothing to eat. Cronies took over sequestered media outfits and big corporations and silenced the press that opted to go underground. The military made warrantless arrests and tortured the militant leaders. Most of them were students and progressive young leaders, some were never to be seen again by their families.

In the countryside, everything seemed normal. In fact, the rebels were despised by the locals and were painted as criminals and lawless elements. The military paraded those they captured and used them for their propaganda, forcing the prisoners to withdraw their support to the uprising by threatening to arrest members of their family.

On the island, there were reported sightings of suspicious people who roamed at night, taking cover in the darkness. Secret lairs in the forest and in the mangroves along the river were attributed to the rebel groups. Some claimed that rebels came in motorized pump boats in the dead of the night with their load of wounded cadres to be hidden in their secret lairs to recuperate. Children were not allowed to play outside beyond eight o'clock in the evening. Windows were closed at nightfall, ever careful not to welcome any stranger. If a visitor came, they were interrogated about the purpose of their visit and the relatives that they knew on the island especially if they don't speak the local language.

Five days later, Tatay came back with Mano Jun's books and other personal belongings. Before coming home, he visited Dada Titay in their old house in Tangulon hoping that Mano Jun had sent word to our aunt. Dada Titay cried upon learning that Mano Jun had left the University in the last semester of his Bachelor of Science in Animal Husbandry course. She had high hopes for him because he was a consistent honor student since elementary school. Mano Jun was expected to be the first one in the family to have a college diploma. Dada Titay's children did not go to college because she could not afford the expenses outside of school fees.

Since then, Tatay drank more often and when he went home, he would instigate a fight with Nanay, threatening to hit anything or anyone on his way. We would cringe on the corner until he was past asleep.

I was inspecting one of Mano Jun's books, looking at the pictures of plants and animals when the postman arrived. Nanay's hands were shaking when she opened the letter, anxious about the news. The letter was from Baba Danding, her younger brother who informed us that Mano Jun was in Manila. With only a map and Baba Danding's address in Las Pinas City, Mano Jun was able to locate their shanty near a dumpsite in Pulang Lupa.

Immediately, Nanay wrote to Mano Jun asking the reason why he left. She pleaded for him to come home and finish his studies. Mano Jun wrote back that he had found a job as a clerk in a government-run warehouse but did not tell us the reason why he left.

Mano Jun would not come home for twenty years and my parents' wish to have a teacher in the family forever vanished.

Mano Fernan, my second oldest brother left for Manila after his high school graduation waiting for his turn to study but because of what Mano Jun did, the others after him were not given the chance. Years later, some of my older siblings bore a resentment to my father for not being able to go to college.

"I could not afford to send another child to college and then leave without a reason." Tatay said.

Nanay was reluctant but she could not disagree openly with Tatay. Mana Jean, Mana Maria and soon Mano Boyet left for Manila too to look for a job. Mana Jean worked in a canteen as a waitress, Mana Maria became a house help somewhere in Valenzuela while Mano Fernan became a mechanic in a big jeepney workshop in Las Pinas. Mana Jean returned home after two years to finish high school and then left again for Manila.

Mano Boyet tried working as a waiter and juggling singing in a bar when the performer could not make it. It was here that he rekindled his love of music. The audience loved his soulful voice and the girls loved his boyish charm. Mano Boyet became an alcoholic so he lost his job at the bar and tried working at the jeepney workshop with Mano Fernan but he was too drunk on some days so he lost his job.

Soon, I forgot their faces. They would not go home even on fiestas. When I was of school age, they would send us notebooks and school supplies at the start of the school year although this only happened on a rare occasion when Nanay pleaded to them after the strong typhoon that left our house roofless. Sometimes they send money orders that Tatay claimed from the post office but again, this seldom happens. They only earn enough for themselves after paying the rent, fare and food. Manila is an expensive city, they tell us. This, I realized years later.

Chapter 6: The Engkantada and Panganahaw

The lambent light of a kerosene lamp glowed on the kitchen window while my sister Daria prepared the family's dinner. On the nearby Pundang, the hornbill took his flight to the mangroves announcing the time and disturbing the bats that scurry out of the caves. At the river bank, Mano Doming checked his traps one last time.

The farmers were returning from the farms after a hard day's work. On their backs were baskets of produce for the family's dinner. Nanay brought sweet potatoes for breakfast while Tatay brought a bayong of plump red macopa from our farm house in Baquiw. It was the season of macopas! My siblings and I picked the juiciest fruits and divided it among ourselves. They were deep crimson and sweet.

In the streets, the shrill voices of children filled the air. This was the best time of the day to play Chinese garter, kaban-kabanay or simply dakup-dakupay. After getting my share of the macopa, I joined my friends in fetching water at the artesian well and filled our earthen jar container to the brim.

Dinner was served. Tatay got his share of the steaming rice and fish stew. Everyone got their share of rice and fish and we ate in silence. Water was passed around. The only sound heard was the clinking of the serving spoon on the rice bowl which was re-filled every so often. Finally, Tatay cleared his throat and everyone came to attention.

"We will take out the weeds in the paddies tomorrow. The irrigation canal and the dikes have to be mended. The weeds are already tall so you have to pull it. In addition, the catch basin of the irrigation canal has to be cleared of debris so that the water flows easily."

Tatay said it to no one in particular but everybody understood to whom they were directed. Water was passed again to everyone and then the dinner was over. I was tasked to wash the dishes. Nanay put back the leftover rice in the pot and blew the embers back to heat the leftover food. This will keep the cat from opening the lid of the pot.

"Any leftover food must be heated so they will not get spoiled. We cannot afford wasting food." Nanay hung the leftover fish stew over the kindling in the hearth.

"Wash the glasses first before the plates so the grease from the plates will not transfer to the glasses."

Nanay ruled the kitchen like Tatay ruled the farm. They did not ask about what we did in school because everyone was expected to do good. Finishing high school was never a question for my parents so when my older sisters came home in the middle of the week, they must have a compelling reason to do so. The secondary school was in the Poblacion and high school students are expected to go home on Friday nights only. My siblings lived with Tata Bala, our maternal grandfather. I did not meet our maternal grandmother because she died long before I was born. I only saw her in the black and white photographs hung in the walls of Tata Bala's house.

I washed the dishes quietly looking out to the rising moon from the kitchen window. It was almost a full moon and I could hear the squealing noise of my friends at the plaza so I quickly finished rinsing the utensils and joined them.

That afternoon at the crossroads near the school and the village, Baba Erling saw a lonesome girl crying by the roadside. She was very fair and beautiful.

"Ineng, why are you crying? Why are you alone at this time of the day? It's already dark. Where do you live? Are you with your parents?"

Baba Erling did not receive any answer from the girl of about eight or nine. She kept on walking until she disappeared in the bend where the big acacias were. Perplexed, he asked around if there were balikbayans with a Caucasian daughter. A village girl marrying a retired American soldier was common on the island. Some girls were forced to work as bar girls in Olongapo City where the US Bases were located so Baba Erling thought that she was the daughter of some village girl married to a Kano. But nobody knew the girl nor had seen her.

"She is an engkantada!" confirmed Mana Sayong with conviction.

Everyone agreed. The story spread like wildfire in the village; not that it was the first time that it happened because it was a regular occurrence to have seen an engkantada, it was deemed as a warning that somebody will be sick because they have hurt her.

"Go home quick! Don't run around because you might hit someone."

Mothers came calling their children to go home but soon the children came back and the plaza was buzzing again with running and shrieking children until it was sleeping time. The village fell into a collective zzzzzz and the kikik glided and hopped from roof to roof checking for pregnant women and sick persons.

That night, I dreamed of eating bread as big as my pillow.

On school days, our cousins Mercedes and Agnes stayed with us so it means having more playmates. Sometimes we would stay up until past bedtime playing jack stone or cards that we made from discarded cigarette boxes. We would only stop when we hear the kikik hovering around the neighborhood. Someone would say the name of the suspected aswang in the village and it would momentarily go away but would return a few minutes later. Then it was sleeping time but everyone crowded in the living room where we rolled the buri mats.

The following night, the moon rose majestically from the east preceded by a light drizzle. I saw it from the kitchen window while cleaning the pots. Instantly, the plaza was alive with children playing.

I was hiding at the back of the stockage when I heard the mothers calling their children again.

"Psst!" "Psst!" It was an urgent call from Mana Mariana's whose way of calling her children has been known in the village. Her "pssst" was persistent and fierce like a matter of life and death.

I reluctantly came out of my hiding place and went to the plaza to check on my friends but they were also dragged home by their mothers so I went home and found my sisters and cousins by the front yard.

"Mano Berting saw the panganahaw. He was peeing in the coconut tree when he looked up to see that it was the legs of the panganahaw." Daria narrated.

"He was so tall that his head towers above the coconuts."

"Wilma, go home." Mana Sayong almost dragged her daughter away.

Instantly, the plaza was abandoned except by old men smoking near the entrance. The stillness of the village was only broken by an occasional barking of dogs.

At the rocky cliff beneath the lighthouse was a natural pool that looked like a giant foot print. To this day, it was believed to be that of the panganahaw so people call it "tunob na si panganahaw" or foot print of panganahaw. People claim that the other foot print was located somewhere on the mainland as the panganahaw could walk across the sea. Although he was a giant, people believe that he did not hurt people. However, people were afraid because of how he looked like: gigantic, dark and bearded.

Since we were not allowed to play outside, Mercedes suggested that we play cards. I fell asleep watching them play because I was afraid of sleeping alone in the room.

Chapter 7: The Storm

Anna was born on the first day of December in 1981. I was six years old and in Grade 1 while Jonas was four. Just like the rest of us, Nanay gave birth at home attended by the *partira*, Mana Babing, who was also my godmother. Mana Babing lived in Sitio Milisbigis, the mountainous area uphill of Sitio Baquiw. Her house was located on a clearing by the roadside with chicken coops and vegetables planted along the fence. She would sometimes bring me a live native chicken on special occasions just like during my Grade 1 graduation where I was third honors.

Nanay was in her mid-40's when Anna was conceived. Dr. Lapuz warned her that the child was *suhi*, so she will have a difficult delivery.

"You have to give birth here in the hospital. You have a very risky delivery." Dr. Lapuz told Nanay. The newly built Capul District Hospital was located in Poblacion.

"Doc, I have delivered eleven children, I can manage this one. This will be the last." Nanay argued.

Tatay was scalding the dressed chicken in the kitchen when Mana Babing rushed out of the room with a worried look. Nanay was unconscious and had no pulse after delivering Anna. Nanay was exhausted and she lost so much blood because Anna took her time. Tatay clutched Nanay's lifeless body in his hands and prayed; probably the only time that he prayed so hard.

. . . ."Lord, I will change for the better if you give me back my wife. Don't let my children be deprived of their mother."

He wept while uttering those words, the only time that we, his children saw him cry. His shoulders were shaking while praying loudly. My older siblings were also crying and had crowded the room. I was too young to understand what was going on but since my siblings were crying, I cried too.

God must have heard the prayer of a remorseful man so He gave him a look of mercy. After about five minutes, Nanay breathed again, opened her eyes and took Anna in her bosom who was wailing loudly. Mana Babing cut her umbilical cord and Tatay buried it beneath the front window and kissed both Nanay and Anna. He ordered one more chicken and a little celebration followed.

Anna had kinky hair and almond-shaped eyes. Her complexion was the color of pale amber and she has a thin shrill voice.

That year, we did not go to the Poblacion to attend the Christmas activities because it had been raining for several days. The wind blew stronger in the afternoon so we stayed indoors. Tatay and Dong tied a rope over to secure the thatched roof. The transistor radio from our neighbor had been broadcasting a new typhoon that would directly hit the province. On Christmas night, Typhoon Dinang ravaged the island. The strong winds shook our house. The typhoon came late in the afternoon which was a blessing because it was still light. It was one of the strongest typhoons that ever battered the island.

I and my other siblings were gathered in the big room with Nanay while Tatay and Dong tied ropes in wooden pegs to save a portion of our roof. We covered ourselves with blankets and mats while the rains poured heavily above us. When the wind went westward, it slowed down a bit. We looked out and realized that the entire roof was gone.

"Let's go to the house of Mana Quilin. Get your changing clothes and some plates. Elsa, bring the pot of rice and viands."

Nanay grabbed the blanket and covered Anna and we ran to Mana Quilin's house which was only three houses away. When we reached the big house, we realized that only Anna's head was covered but her feet were exposed to the wind and rain.

We brought out our dinner of rice and dried fish and ate with the other families that have taken shelter in Mana Quilin's house just as several typhoons passed. The other neighbors had evacuated ahead of us so we settled in one corner along with the other four families. Tatay and Dong followed before the winds grew stronger again, dripping wet after securing what remained of our house. For us children, this was an opportunity to play while the adults pressed their ears in the diminishing sound of the transistor radio to wait for updates about the storm.

As far as I remembered, most typhoons started somewhere in Borongan or Guiuan in the eastern part of Samar Island. The typhoon would travel to the northern or western part of Samar and then gather strength in the seas before it hit the Islands of Catanduanes, Masbate or Polilio in Quezon or goes north to Aurora. The storm almost always exits in the western or northern part of the Philippines. The elders would update us about the direction and location of the wind so we knew when the rains would stop.

While in the evacuation house, we played hide and seek in the rooms while the winds lashed out the trees outside. The windows and doors were smashed so the adults covered them with plywood.

In the morning, the sun shone again although it was still cloudy. The coconuts and other trees fell everywhere which means that there were plenty of fruits to eat. The sea shore was covered with drift woods and other trash from the mountains and probably from other islands. The water was murky which was perfect for *panabay* so my sisters and I got our old mosquito net and pushed it on the shallow waters. We got some *balanak*, shrimps and crabs so we had something for lunch and supper.

When the typhoon was over, most of our roof was missing. The kitchen and the two smaller rooms at the back were totally wrecked. Miraculously, the living room and the roof of the fireplace were intact together with the wooden floor. All our clothes were drenched while the other household items were strewn all over the house. The pots and pans were scattered while the pig in the sty shuddered in the cold. We tried to restore the house by putting together whatever we could find. The other houses suffered as badly. Our neighbor's whole roof was sitting on top of the talisay tree near the swamp about fifty yards away so that it looked like a tree house. The waves smashed the houses along the shore and the river swelled washing ashore vegetables along the bank.

The chapel was only one house away and was along our way from Mana Quilin's. The roof of the chapel near the altar was also blown off and some of the pews were wrecked.

Nanay and the other devotees were cleaning in the chapel when they noticed something.

"Luning, look at Our Lady, her dress has amorsiko!" Mana Juling gasps.

"Oh, she's wet. She's not in her usual place in her niche!" Nanay observed.

"There is mud in her dress and she's wet. Oh my God, she's been out in the storm!" Mana Elba was on the verge of tears. "Dandoy said he saw a beautiful woman chasing the waves away at the bay during the storm. That must be our De Salvacion!"

The other devotees crossed themselves and everyone started saying the rosary.

This story will be repeated over and over again in the next few weeks. Although, it was not the first time that such a miracle was attributed to Our Lady, especially during storms that has become a yearly occurrences.

Our patron saint, the Nuestra Senora de Salvacion is considered as the patron saint of travellers. People leaving the island visit her chapel before their journey to ask for protection. Nanay was one of those that people sought to perform the *patumban* to protect them on their journey.

Dong gathered *umbot* from the fallen coconuts that Nanay cooked with the shrimp and crabs that we caught. The fish were cooked in vinegar as paksiw.

We salvaged anything that we could and rebuilt the house. The new house was much smaller and lower than the previous one to avoid it being blown away by the next typhoons. Several typhoons visit our island every year along with the monsoon rains so it is more practical to build lower houses.

The following year, Nanay became the Hermana Mayor for the Barangay Fiesta. It was part of Tatay's promise of change and a thanksgiving for Nanay's second life. We butchered two pigs and a young carabao for the guests. Tatay also ordered crabs from his cousin who owned a fish pond which was served to the archbishop, the priest, the mayor and other special guests. During the vesper night dance, Nanay and Tatay danced the Kuracha, the only time that I saw them dancing together.

On the feast day, the Archbishop performed the High Mass along with the Parish Priest.

Before the fiesta, Nanay wrote to my older brothers and sisters in Manila to go home but for one reason or another, none of them could come. It had been several years since they left and they have not returned home.

In fact, I did not know my other older siblings until I was around nine years old since I was still too young when they left.

Every year, there was an exodus of young people leaving the island for the city to work as house helps, stevedores and factory workers. My older brothers and sisters were no exception. During summer, they come back to celebrate the fiesta in the third week of May. A few days before the fiesta, the motorboats from Matnog were loaded with balikbayans with fairer complexions, ready to show the village people their new-found status. They would speak Tagalog even at home or Inabaknon with a Tagalog accent. Some have found husbands or wives from other regions but most others prefer to marry our own.

I heard that most of them were working in the market in Divisoria particularly in Bilbao Street where the boys were hired as porters for the delivery of fruits and vegetables from Baguio and Quezon province. Others worked as factory workers in Cubao, Novaliches, Bulacan or Pasig and they rented a room in Malanday, Marikina, Sapang Palay in Bulacan or in Sta. Cruz, Manila. Later on, their shanties were demolished and they were given relocation in Dasmarinas Cavite but continued to work in Bilbao. Those who could not carry heavy loads sell plastic clothes hangers, kitchen utensils and other household items. Still others worked as stay-in house helpers in exclusive gated subdivisions of Corinthian Village, Valle Verde or Forbes Park. One of my friends became the maid of a popular young star who regaled us with stories about tapings for television shows and shootings for movies. There were no television sets nor movie houses on the island during that time so I could not imagine what she was talking about. Electricity was only available in the town when I was in high school and I was able to watch canned television shows and movies in betamax format that was shown at night for a fee of P1.00 or P2.00 per person.

The balikbayans brought biscuits in tin cans along with condiments for the fiesta together with new clothes for the family members so I envied my friends more.

Every year, I would crane my neck to check if any of my siblings were among the passengers of the overloaded boat but I always left the dock disappointed. Nanay and Tatay expected them too but they did not show their dismay.

And so I came to regard them as distant relatives that I only knew through the pictures they sent enclosed in the intermittent letters they wrote. When I was around ten years old, Nanay would ask me to respond to their letters. They said they are pleased that I can write and speak Tagalog even at a young age. After a typhoon, I would write letters informing them of the situation: the house needed repair, the coconuts were destroyed and would bear no fruit until after another year. Sometimes they send us money through the postal services. But because they only had enough, they could only send so much.

Chapter 8: Two storms

My parents were married when they were 21 and 22 years old respectively. It was considered late during the time. They settled in Sitio Baquiw in the land owned by Nanay's cousins. This cousin opted to transfer to the University town when their children started going to college.

"You will have a fairly good married life. You will experience hardships but you will also receive good graces. You will have many children and you and your husband will race each other to old age. However you will go through two major storms in your life as a married couple" the fortune teller told Nanay after their wedding on January 29, 1957.

The fortune teller was a young woman from Leyte who married Nanay's distant cousin.

"That is life's supposed to be right? Nanay countered. "I don't expect a good life because I married a landless man so there will always be hardships."

The woman checked Nanay's hands one more time and traced the lines in both her palms. "You can counter any bad luck with prayers."

Nanay bore her eldest child, a son, after a year. The second child, another son was born two years after and then two daughters, one after the other. When she was pregnant with the fifth child, she experienced nausea more often and thought she saw other people surrounding her. In the middle of the night, she would hear voices and she had difficulty sleeping.

Ella was born on a rainy day in August, weak and frail. The *partira* had to slap her buttocks harder before she cried for the first time. Worried, the people around forgot to say "you're mine" until a little bit later.

Ella had kinky jet-black hair, the color of midnight. She grew up to be very timid but she was compassionate to all, people, animals or even to the plants. She refused to step on the plants as she went along the mountain trail picking wild fruits, ever careful not to hurt the plants. She talked to them apologizing that she had to pick their fruits.

One day, she came across a newly hatched dove that fell from its nest from the branch of the cotton tree in the backyard. She carefully picked the hapless bird and put it back on its nest while its mother hovered around her suspiciously.

Her dainty steps irritated the living wits of the spirits living on the old lauan tree on the western side of the house. That was the explanation of Tata Bala when he fumigated the house with incense and melted a candle in a plate with water. Her fever would not subside after five days.

"The engkanto wants to marry Ella because she is very ladylike. He is irritated by her dainty movements but at the same time, he likes her so much that he wants to take her to his palace". Tata Bala takes a closer look at the shape of the melted candle in the plate half-filled with water.

"What do we do?" asked Nanay worriedly.

"Let us offer a white young chicken, the one that has not laid eggs, candies and cigarettes to appease the engkanto."

Tata Bala paced around the room checking Ella's forehead and then looking at the direction of the lauan tree.

Ella did not recover from her fever. She was brought to the hospital in Allen town the following day and was brought back in a wooden casket after three days. I was four years old. Many people came. Some were crying while I was wondering what was going on. Ella was buried at the municipal cemetery after three days. She was eleven years old.

I have this faint memory of Ella in our farmhouse gently pushing my hammock as she sang a melody. I could not remember her face anymore. Her classmate showed me a picture of Ella in her green Girl Scout uniform during the school-wide Jamboree when she was in Grade 4. She was serious while looking at the camera. *Mawawaraon*, someone who is most likely to die young, remarked her classmate.

I did not know my birthday until I was around nine years old. We did not celebrate birthdays since we could not afford it. I was born two years after Elsa, who came after Dong. Mano Boyet was born on a full moon which explained his vanity according to Nanay. Daria was born one year after Mano Boyet. They are the siblings that I grew up with although Mano Boyet and Daria also left for Manila to work after their high school graduation but Daria eventually returned home after one year and then married her high school boyfriend.

Chapter 9: The Younger Children

Nanay tried taking pills after her seventh child. She was *surundon*. However, she felt nauseated after taking pills. Nanay also began having headaches and other discomforts so she stopped. And so she bore twelve children all in all.

I am the tenth child. I started schooling at four years old when the village midwife put out a kindergarten school on the second floor of our relative's house. In addition, Nanay taught me the alphabet while my sisters taught me how to read and write. When my sisters were not looking, I got their pencils and scribbled the alphabet on the bedroom wall. There were earlier writings on the wall but I did not know what they were until I learned how to read. They were the names of my older brothers and sisters.

Unfortunately, my kindergarten class was interrupted because the midwife resumed his classes at the University to finish Nursing. He was a Barangay scholar. In return, he rendered his free services in the Barangay which he did with so much passion. He returned after he finished his Nursing degree and passed the board exam. Later on, he worked abroad so I did not see him for a long time. Until we meet again accidentally several years later, when I already graduated and worked on my first job as a researcher.

At five years old, I was too young to be enrolled in Grade 1 so I envied my older friends who were in school. I watched them from the window when they got home from school at noon. I really wanted to go to school but I was not seven yet.

The following year, I tagged along with Elsa to her class partly because no one would look for me at home. Elsa was in Grade 3 and the Grade 1 pupils were in the next room where some of my friends were enrolled. I was curious so I peeped at the window to check what they were doing. When they were reading the alphabet and the numbers from the board which I already learned, I read aloud with them. The teacher, Mrs. Bandal, who lived five houses away from us noticed that I can read better than the other students in the class so she invited me in as a visitor.

"Get inside. Would you like to sit in?"

"Yes." I said timidly.

Since then, I would go directly to her classroom while Elsa was in the next room. We would take our lunch at home and I would return even before the bells because I wanted to play with my new classmates. At the end of the year, I was awarded an orange ribbon as the third best pupil while Elsa was valedictorian for the third straight year.

During the graduation ceremonies, the grade 1 pupils were assigned to read the acrostic and I was assigned as the first reader. Our parts were written at the back of the cut-out letters but I made sure I memorized mine so I looked straight to the audience and confidently recited:

"Araw-araw kami ay pumapasok sa paaralan (Everyday, we go to school)." There were murmurs and then some crackling laughter from the audience but I went on until I was done with my part.

Ngiwit. That's what people call me because I could not pronounce the letter "r" correctly. I have a lisp that even until today, I could not pronounce some English sounds properly. But that did not discourage me in any way. Even as early as six years old, I was sure of one thing: to finish my studies.

The following year, I was officially enrolled in Grade 2. My new teacher was a spinster, Ms. Jesusa. She likes me because I can memorize poems fast and can read fast. I wanted to become an astronaut after reading "The Distance to Andromeda". I wanted to see the stars and to travel to space.

I was a consistent honor student although I was not a diligent student. I was shy and would not raise my hand voluntarily but my teachers called me anyway. In grade 5, I got one of the two top honors together with my cousin Maribel who was the class valedictorian since grade one.

In my final year in elementary, I got the highest honor and academic awards in English, Filipino and Social Studies. Truth be told, I struggled in Math.

As I took the podium for my valedictory address, I looked beyond the familiar faces, into the shore and beyond the islands in the horizon thinking, I want to be someone that people will look up to just like my first teacher.

Nanay felt that she was luckier with us younger children because we excel in school and we didn't give her so much headaches so she did not regret having us.

Every summer, Tatay cut my hair very short like a military man. I would sit still until he finished shaving the sides of my head lest I would hear his "Tsk! Tsk! Task!" and the possibility of cutting my ears with his very sharp *labaha*. If I had my way, I would have wanted my hair a little bit longer and not the military look he insisted on me and my younger brother Jonas. I still remember the sensation of my hair falling on my back and the sound of the shaver as it glided on my head like cloth being torn apart.

Being an islander, everyone knew how to swim. It is a survival skill for anyone living on the island. I learned to swim on my own just like other boys and girls my age. Summers also mean high tide so children played in the mouth of the river and jumped from the wooden bridge. This is how I learned how to swim, by imitating the older boys. When the pump boat arrived, we would race to get to its outriggers and ogle at the passengers inside.

After lunch, we were required to sleep at siesta time. Nanay would sing us love songs to lull us to sleep. Nanay sang a variety of songs in Inabaknon, Waray, Cebuano or even Bikol. Nanay didn't have a beautiful voice which I inherited. In fact, she had a tentative and shaky voice but nevertheless, she could carry a tune. I always look forward to her songs because the only other time that I heard her sing was when she was drinking coconut wine with the other farmers at the end of the farming season.

Even now, I could hear her sing "Kun Ako Aglimot Mo" (If You Forget Me)

Ako aglimot mo
Si tang'nga na si adda gugma mo
Kun sangom nag-intom
I kasakitan dimuan
Sing'nga na may hamok
Paan'na ko i pag-antos
Kun ambanan mo ako
I kasakitan dimuan
Antos k okay nagpumwan

Si kalaluman na si sangom
Gana lain nag-intom ko
Kundi i mga allingon mo
Ngan malab'bat huwang ta
Agpamati siray i bulan
I burak, i bituon pa.

Agpalipay mo ako
Agpabido mo ako
Bisan ako aglimot mo.

You forgot me
In the midst of our love
At night I remember
All I have gone through
Where will I put
My sufferings

If you leave me
All the pain
I will endure
In the middle of the night
I remember nothing
But the things you say to me
When we were with company
The moon was witness
Even the flowers and the stars.

You made me happy
You made me sad
Then you forsake me

Sensing that Nanay was asleep, I snuck out of the house and went with my friends to pick guava near the rice fields in Malpal. One summer day, Levi suggested that we check the *lamon-lamon* along the sea shore.

"Oh, there have been others who came ahead." I blurted out upon seeing the torn vines.

"Look, ripe fruits on that vine." Marlon started climbing while the others looked for more fruits. Although disappointed that we were not the first to pick the fruits, we got a handful from our forage and left a trail of red and orange peel on the sandy road.

Elsa and Daria were already up when Nanay gently woke me up.

It was still dark outside and the crickets from the breadfruit tree made a momentary stop when I got out the kitchen door to the toilet at the back to pee. A few fireflies hovered around the tree like dim Christmas lights. I filled my cup of rice coffee and boiled sweet potato by adjusting my eyes to the dimming kerosene lamp. We ate in silence. Afterwards, each of us grabbed our rattan baskets and flat-tipped bolo. On the way out, I put on my straw hat and exited through the kitchen door.

Nanay wrapped the left-over sweet potato and dried fish cooked in the embers. The leaves of the gumamela were wet with dew and the morning star was still high on the eastern horizon when we set out to the sea. The water had completely subsided when we reached Kagasangan. On the horizon, the kerosene lamps looked like low hanging stars scattered along the ocean.

By dawn, almost everyone in the village was stooping their backs gathering *gulaman*.

I found a handful of lush gulaman on some corals at the puddles and tide pools. I turned the big rocks and found edible shells under them and tried to catch the small fishes by hitting them with my bolo. Around nine o'clock, the tide was getting back so we retreated to the shore. All of us had their baskets full of gulaman, shellfish and some *lato*.

After harvest, the gulaman is blanched until they turn green. Then it is dried under the sun and washed every now and then until they are bleached white, then it is ready to sell. The price per kilogram was ten to fifteen pesos depending on the supply and quality.

Almost everyone in the village old enough to pick gulaman was engaged in the trade. This season lasted for a few days every month especially from August to December and from March to May when the low tide was extremely low.

The gulaman season came after the rice harvest season. Some villagers would embark on a fishing trip to the nearby island of Ticao, in Masbate province where gulaman was abundant. Locals don't harvest it as much as we did in Capul. While the men go spear fishing, women harvest gulaman. They would stay for a week or two until they have enough money to bring home to their families.

We would reserve the best gulaman for the fiesta in May. This is how we process gulaman into gelatin from my memory:

    1. Clean the gulaman by removing the small corals and other weeds and soak in fresh water for at least an hour.

    2. Boil the fresh gulaman (around one fourth kilo) with the leaves of *batwan* until they turn soft and sloppy.

3. Strain the mixture so that only the liquefied particles are left.

4. Boil the liquid gulaman again and add sugar, milk or other flavors based on your preference. Strain again when transferring in decorative containers and cool down.

5. Chill overnight before serving.

Chapter 10: Kapidos & Luning

My grandfather, Francisco Castillo was a Spanish Mestizo, the son of a Spaniard and a local maiden. My older siblings called him Tata Iling. Tata Iling's family owned vast tracts of land in Capul and in the neighboring town of San Isidro where his family originally came from. They were a political clan of sorts with Tata Iling serving as Capitan Del Barrio of San Luis during the post-war. Baba Amboy, Tatay's older brother, was also Capitan for several terms when elections were still held manually with secret ballots. However, their tracts of land were eventually sold because of the vices of the male members of the family. They would wager the land titles when left with no money in the cockfight.

The family was known to have a bad temper and were always grumpy and irritable especially when they lost in the cock fight. Hence, they were called "Kapidos".

Tatay did not inherit Tata Iling's height and meztiso looks although some of my uncles and cousins were tall and had aquiline nose. Two of Tatay's siblings remain in Barrio Tangulon, in San Isidro town where they were born but they would attend the fiesta in San Luis were the four other siblings settled including Tatay. Most of my uncles became farmers after they lost all their properties to cockfighting, therefore became dark complexioned too although some of my cousins had fair complexion and were no doubt good looking. I, on the other hand look a lot like my mother: dark complexioned, wide nosed and plump although I was skinny as a boy.

I don't have any memory of my paternal grandmother because she died before I was born but I do remember a bit about Tata Iling because I was around four years old when he died. He was called *Allen Allen* by the people in the village because he always wanted to go home to Tangulon every time the motorboats left for Allen town. Allen is the port town and the entryway to Tangulon. My older siblings did not want to eat together with Tata Iling because he didn't want to wash his whole hands, only his fingertips because according to him that's the only part of his hands that touches the food anyway. So when lunchtime comes, one of them would go out and shout "Allen! Allen!" and Tata Iling would immediately clutch his bag and rush towards the dock. Some of my cousins live near the dock and when they see Tata Iling gushing about the motorboat, they would say that it left just minutes ago.

"Why, you are slow Tata Iling. You see, the boat has left just now." Mano Jim would say.

"Look at the tail, it has turned into Kagasangan." Mano Efren would add pointing to a fishing boat.

Of course, my cousins knew about the script and when Tata Iling came back, my siblings were done eating. Since then, Tata Iling earned the moniker. He died at the ripe age of 89.

My maternal grandfather, Tata Bala came from a family of faith healers. During Holy Week, he and some other *albularyo* prayed and fasted inside a secret cave and came out more "powerful". He had a deep knowledge on medicinal plants that he grew on the big yard around our ancestral house in the Poblacion. His kitchen was an apothecary. People came to him for common ailments like cough, cold, flu and even those who break their bones during a bad fall. Other than this, Tata Bala knew if a patient was hit by an engkanto or just naturally sick with flu. He would feel the patient's pulse and he knew right away what ailed the patient and recommended the plants to be administered: seven young leaves of guava, seven young leaves of star apple, *clavo*, *herbabuena*, bark of a certain tree, etc. The leaves or the bark and roots facing east should be harvested but the plant should not be cut dead otherwise the illness would not go away.

During the Japanese Invasion, Tata Bala's family evacuated to the mountainous part of Barangay Sawang with other families. Tata Bala owned land in this part that Nanay would visit when I was a boy until this was sold to a relative. During the war, they harvested wild roots like *ba'ay* and *ad'dut* to survive while they waited for their crops to bear fruits.

Ad'dut is actually a poisonous root but the locals learned the process of removing the toxin by peeling and slicing it thinly and submerging it in running water, preferably in the brook or creek for a few days. Then it is sun dried and cooked in coconut milk and sugar. Tata Bala also grew sugarcane while hiding in the mountains. The sugarcane was squeezed with the help of a wooden machine run by a carabao. The juice was cooked in a big cauldron until sticky then transferred to an empty coconut shell. The sugarcane cakes lasted for several months. Some were made into candies.

Nanay had four sisters and three brothers. Being the female among the middle children, she was assigned to care after my grandmother who suffered from diabetes. Nanay only finished elementary school. Nang Titay did not live long to see her other grandchildren. I only saw her in a framed photograph hung in one of the posts of Tata Bala's house which would later become a big part of my young adult life.

Tata Bala was around 70 years old when I was in grade school. Me and my siblings together with our cousins from other Barangays would converge in his house during special occasions like fiestas or if there were gatherings in the high school where my older siblings were studying like during the Junior and Senior Prom or during their graduation.

During the lull months of the farming seasons, Tatay gathered coconut wine that we sold to the neighborhood store at P12.00 per gallon. Early in the morning, Tatay collected the fresh sap of the coconut flower that he cut the day before. The young flower was bent and tied at the tip with a coconut shell to gather the sap. The sap was collected in a *hungot* or bamboo container slung by the *manang'giti* in his shoulder. The mouth of the *hungot* was covered by a mesh netting to protect the wine from insects and to sift it when transferred to the bottles.

The coconut sap was mixed with *baruk*, a bark of mangrove to enhance the color and flavor of *tuwak* before it was sold. When aged and distilled, *tuwak* become *bahal* or *bahalina*. To produce a *bahalina*, the *tuwak* was distilled by transferring it to a different earthen jar container every few days, covered and kept in a dark part of the house. Otherwise, the wine turns into vinegar when exposed to sunlight.

I was assigned to sell the *tuwak* to the store and buy Tatay a pack of La Campana, a cheap cigarette without a butt.

A few months before the fiesta, Tatay would start gathering *tuwak* for his guests. When he became drunk, he turned boisterous and cantankerous until he fall asleep. In high school, I was embarrassed to invite my friends at home even on fiestas because Tatay was rowdy when drunk.

Tatay's drunken ways was one of the reasons why my older siblings left and would not go home according to Nanay. When my two oldest brothers where younger, they would carry Tatay from the adjacent hill to our house. Tatay would call from the top of the hill and then sleep by the roadside.

Although Tatay was a drunkard, he was one hard working father who made sure that we had food on the table every day. He worked all day in the farm with Nanay. His only vice was drinking which he could not control at times. In the sunset years of his life, Tatay actually changed for the better and stopped drinking. He even joined Nanay's Bible group and became a devout Catholic.

"The Moros are coming and they will kidnap young children. You will be taken inside a sack and you will be offered as a sacrifice when they construct big buildings and bridges."

That was what our elders told us when we refused to sleep in the afternoon. Passing motorboats in the afternoon was not very common so when we heard the distant sound of motorboats passing along the bay, we would scamper back home and sleep.

In fact, the oral lore of our family is rooted in the Moro Raids during the early years of Spanish conquest in the 1600's until the early 18th century.

The aborigines of the island were called the Agta. They were short but stout, dark complexioned and had kinky hair. They were hunters and gatherers and they lived in caves.

In the early 13th century, a group of sea borne immigrants from Sabah, Malaysia settled in the island. They were led by their ruler named Abak who left Sabah to resist the rule of their king. Later on, they intermarried with the locals until the Agtas became part of the minorities and were eventually wiped out. In fact, when I was growing up, people referred to the Agtas as supernatural beings like the *engkantos* because they were rarely seen and they lived in the remaining forested areas of the island. People feared them although they didn't harm anyone. Later on, the Agtas became part of the stories told by our elders.

The Spaniards came in the early 1600's and made the island the center of Christianity in the whole of Samar provinces. The limestone church which is still standing is a testament to that era. The locals became Catholics. Later on, the Galleon ships from Butuan in Mindanao would pass by the island before they continued sailing to Acapulco Mexico through the San Bernardino Strait. The San Bernadino Strait is a perilous passage and it was believed that a few Galleon ships met their untimely end in the sea which is the gateway to the Pacific Ocean.

Before continuing their journey, the Galleon ships would take refuge at the rocky beach in the north-western part of the island and take some provisions. One of the sailors carved the name "Acapulco" in the rocks, and people refer to that part as Acapulco. Later on, the name was corrupted and became the official name of the whole island hence the island is now officially known as Capul. However, some locals still call the island as Abak until now in deference to the first chieftain. We also call ourselves Abaknon and our language as Inabaknon.

The Castillos are one of the biggest clans on the island. In one local election, a relative who ran for the provincial council traced our family history to introduce himself to our relatives. According to him, the present Castillos are descendants of Esperanza, a beautiful maiden and one of the great granddaughters of Datu Abak himself.

As a *binukot*, Esperanza was treated like a princess. She was not assigned any household chores and she was carried on a hammock whenever she went around the village on rare occasions.

In one of the Moro raids, Esperanza was abducted and she never returned to the island.

Several years later, a young man arrived on the island who introduced himself to be one of the sons of Esperanza. People remember Esperanza and the family celebrated the return of one of her sons.

According to her son, she was treated well by her captors and married the son of a Muslim datu. Her son later embraced Christianity and adopted the surname Castillo and settled permanently in the island. He married a local girl and became the ancestors of the present Castillo clan.

Our family history has another binukot. Her name was Milagros, the younger sister of Tata Bala. Nang Milagros was schooled in the old tradition of learning the lore of our ancestors from the songs, stories, dances and the magical incantations for different ceremonies particularly the individual's rites of passage; from birth, growing up, marriage and even death. The *binukots* of old were considered as a sort of nobility because they were direct descendants of the *datus* who ruled the islands of Samar and those of neighboring islands in the Visayas and Mindanao.

Nang Milagros was a beauty sought by young men. When she was of age for marriage, her parents demanded a big dowry consisting of a big tract of land, farm animals, jewelries, expensive fabrics and a house. Many suitors came to ask for her hand in marriage who offered to give her more but she refused.

Until a dashing young man from mainland Samar, the new *parolista* came to the island and enthralled the young *binukot* with his guitar skills. They fell in love and the wedding was set. The celebration lasted a week. It was the most lavish wedding that the island had ever known.

The newlyweds settled near the lighthouse on the north western tip of the island and produced beautiful children. The ladies were wooed by the most eligible bachelors in town as well as from other neighboring islands. But the young men had to wait for the ladies to become teachers before they could marry.

Nanay's cousins studied in the University while she took care of her ailing mother. I did not meet Nanang Titay, Tata Bala's wife, because she died of diabetes before I was born. Nanay married the son of a landless farmer and took over the farmlands of her relatives while her cousins became doctors, engineers and teachers.

On the summer of my ninth birthday, Nanay took me to gather mussels in Sitio Malpal. We walked the three kilometer sandy road in the blistering summer sun, stopping twice along the way to knock on some relatives to ask for water.

We arrived early and the water had not receded completely so Nanay took me up to the lighthouse. It was the first time that I saw the lighthouse up close. Before this, I only saw the distant shaft of revolving light on clear nights from our window. This time, another family, a distant relative of Nanay, had been taking care of the lighthouse.

We asked permission from the guard to go up the tower. Nanay led me to the spiral steel staircase until we reached the porch. High above the tower, Nanay coaxed me to look outside. My feet were shaking because I was afraid of heights, so Nanay held me tightly as I struggled to balance myself. The wind hurt my face but I could see the sea below slowly receding and the gulaman gatherers had started collecting their harvest. The islands on the other side of the sea were staring at me like a threat. Mt. Bulusan looked so near and I felt that I could jump over the adjacent islands.

"Your Nang Titay comes from a small village near Mt. Bulusan. She used to point it to us up here in the tower when we were young." It was the first time that I heard of such a story. I always thought Nang Titay was a local. No wonder, there are only a few Amaros in Capul and they were all our close relatives.

"How did Tata Bala and Nang Titay meet?" I inquired.

"Your Tata Bala was selling copra in Bulan while your Nang Titay was selling vegetables in the *tabu-an*." The *tabu-an* was a temporary market held once a week usually on a Saturday where farmers and other local producers sell their produce. Nanay pointed out where Bulan was but it was not visible because the port town was covered by the other islands.

"They soon became sweethearts after a few more chance meetings in the *tabuan*. After their wedding, they settled on the island and produced eight children. I am the fifth."

The view from the top of the lighthouse was exhilarating. Looking out from the tower I realized for the first time that our island was small and only one among the many islands in this part and that there were other places that were bigger. I imagined them to be grander, with tall buildings and fast cars; something that we did not have in the island. That early, I wanted to explore those islands and travel to different places. I wanted to travel the world. A passenger boat passed by the San Bernardino Strait and I could see the people inside wondering where they came from and where they were going.

What were the other places especially in the mainland?

The wind blew harder so we decided to descend the tower. Nanay thanked the *Parolista* for letting us up the tower. Going back, we took the shortcut passing through the house of a classmate whose family was a fisherman. They were preparing their net, mending the torn parts in their *bungsaran* when Nanay and I passed by and they exchanged pleasantries. The tide had completely receded when we started gathering mussels. Mussels grow among corals and in the sandy parts of the sea bed. Some weeds have grown on the mussels so they were easy to spot.

Every now and then, I would look at the passing ships along the strait; some were carrying cargoes while others had passengers with orange-colored life vests wandering in the decks. The passenger boats returned at lunchtime and only the smaller fishing boats were gliding in the rolling waves near the end of the surf where I got a few conches.

We gathered a basketful and cleaned them before we retraced our steps back to the village at dusk.

Later that night, we enjoyed the mussels cooked in coconut milk and we had enough until lunch the following day.

Chapter 11: The Vanishing Island

Checking my splintered hand, I stood on a boulder and looked out the horizon. It was a clear day. I had to finish covering the pechay seedlings with banana trunks before the sun became too hot. The distant islands looked like Chinese paintings with different hues of blue and gray. In the middle of the San Bernardino Strait was an islet that was not visible during high tide. People say nobody can get into the island because the nearer one gets, the farther it becomes.

"Did you hurt your hand?" Nanay was behind me while I was holding my left hand.

"It's not that bad. I got a splinter in my left thumb while pulling the weed." I was able to pull the thorn out immediately but a small pool of blood was oozing from it.

"You have to be careful. Wash your hands with clean water so that your wound will not get infected." Nanay said and returned to her work.

I stabbed the blunt bolo on the ground so I could get back to it afterwards and went down to the brook nearby to wash my hands and get more water and continued what I was doing.

"In life, you have two choices, to wield a bolo or a pen." Nanay sensed that I was not too keen on farm work.

"You can see me and your Tatay, how hard we work on the farm because this is the only livelihood that we know. We will die tilling the soil but you can be more if you want."

I looked at the island again but heavy clouds blocked my vision of it. I wondered what it looked like and if anybody lived there. Some say, it was the place of the *engkantos* and only those befriended by them can go to the island.

I continued with my work, pulling the weeds and cultivating the edges of the vegetables and taking out the worms eating the leaves of the eggplant that had started to bloom. The chili plants and the okra had started flowering..

"You will not get hungry as long as you know how to till the land. It may not always be a good harvest but the earth will never fail you as long as you work." Nanay continued. "Don't do as our indolent neighbors do who would ask for malunggay leaves but don't plant the branch that I gave them. They want to eat but they don't want to work." Nanay shakes her head.

Nanay plucked out the worm from the chili leaves and buried them in the ground.

"You have to take care of your plants so that they will yield good fruits. Plants are like children, you have to take care of them while they are young. Once they start bearing fruits you can have a good harvest but you have to keep the parasites away.

I look at Nanay's sturdy build, her plump but strong hips swaying as she climbs the slopes. Childbirth has not slowed her. She moved among the rows of vegetables plucking weeds and worms, inspecting the leaves and cultivating the base so that the water would be easily absorbed by the plants. I went in the opposite direction and inspected the plants. I froze when I saw a gigantic worm dangling at the back of the okra leaf. My hair stood on end but I confronted the parasite by poking it with the end of my bolo then stabbed it and buried it in the ground, the soft body cut in half.

Chapter 12: Elma and Elmo

There was a century-old Acacia tree near the main entrance of the elementary school with a gaping hole at its base. We used to play on the Bermuda grass around it during recess but we were warned not to make so much noise especially during lunch time.

People wondered why the tree was not cut when the concrete fence was constructed when in fact it grew along the fence line. Some people claimed to have seen a palace-like house in its place instead of a hapless tree. Others claimed to have seen dwarves frolicking near it at sunset and the sound of kitchen utensils at meal time.

The Acacia was not the only tree in the campus believed to be inhabited by mystical beings which were mostly elementals according to the shaman. At the back of the classrooms were century-old breadfruit trees which were believed to be inhabited by spirits of the dead taken by the *engkantos*. During meal times, inhabitants near the school claimed to have heard the noise of slamming kitchen utensils and then loud voices of people eating or celebrating. However, children as we were, we climbed its trunks and settled on its branches, oblivious of what people warned us.

There were two shallow fish ponds framed with riprap at the back of the school buildings and an open well where we draw water for our plants. The ground was planted with Bermuda grass where we played during recess and lunch breaks. There was no other entertainment during this time other than the radio and children preferred to play in the school grounds before the classes started. I used to play softball with my classmates using a woven coconut leaf as ball, *shatom* or skipping rope in this part of the campus. We pulled the vines growing along the riprap fence for our rope.

Nikka was not always called to any of the games so she pretended to have an imaginary friend in the form of a green lizard that she caught in the trunk of a coconut tree. Her right point finger and middle finger were joined so in effect she only had four fingers in her right hand and it freaked us out.

"It's okay if you don't pick me on your side. I can play with my friend."

"You have no friends. You only have four fingers."

"Look! This is my friend." Nikka showed us the green lizard from her pocket and we scampered away.

She proceeded to play with her pet lizard, talking to it like a person and she pretended that it respond to her. Nikka continued talking to her imaginary friend during recess and lunch break so the other children kept away from her.

In July of that year, our teacher Mrs. Dela Cruz gave birth to her youngest child. When she resumed teaching, she employed a nanny for Earl, her youngest child.

Elma was from Mondragon town, the town after the University town of Catarman. She was about sixteen years old and a dusky beauty. Every morning, Elma brought Earl inside the campus and played under the canopied breadfruit trees. Mrs. Dela Cruz's house was right outside the riprap wall of the school. That morning, we could hear Elma's crisp laughter from our homeroom. We did not mind her because we knew she was babysitting Earl.

That night, Elma went missing. Later on, she was heard screaming from one of the rooms inside the house. She was trembling and sweating like she just came from a faraway place.

"Go away! I don't want to go with you anymore!" she said to an invisible person.

"We're not bad people. We won't take you anywhere." Baba Erling was calming Elma.

"He's here! He's here! Please hide me! I don't want to go with him!" she crawled to the corner as if hiding from somebody. She wrestled everyone who wanted to hold her but even the six men combined could not pin her down.

When she fell asleep, she was brought to Baba Erling's house on the other side of the village. The old men guarded the house while the family was evacuated. Not long after, they were attacked by somebody with rocks thrown from every direction even though all the windows and doors were closed. Fortunately, nobody was hit.

Meanwhile, at Baba Erling's house, they heard someone knocking loudly on the door. When they opened it, no one was there. Suddenly, Elma started screaming at an invisible person.

"I don't want to go with you anymore! No! Don't come near me! I will jump outside the window if you come near!" Her blood shot eyes were like sharp daggers that could pierce a person dead.

Six men held Elma while she struggled but she was very strong and was able to get loose. She ran to the kitchen then to the other rooms and back again, screaming at someone. She momentarily calmed down but was disturbed all night long so the people could not rest.

Mano Delfin, the *albularyo* came early in the morning. Before he entered the house, he claimed to be stopped by an unseen force. He performed some incantations but every now and then, Elma would scream and shout at an invisible person. The situation did not improve for several days and Elma became weak. She would not eat.

Full moon came and the village waited in anticipation as Mano Delfin performed the ritual of *pagbawi*. People gathered inside the elementary school to witness it. Out of nowhere, Elmo allegedly appeared on horseback, wearing an all-white ensemble and riding a white horse. An ex-CAFGU, a neighbor of Mrs. Dela Cruz allegedly shot Elmo but the slugs stopped before they hit him then he disappeared in thin air.

The albularyo felt defeated. Elma's condition was getting worse by the day so Mrs. Dela Cruz decided to bring her back to her hometown. While passing through Igang, the boat crew heard shouts of celebration complete with a brass band and festive noise. Elma was reunited with her family but within the she passed on and people believed that she was taken by the *engkantos*.

Mano Delfin the *albularyo* suggested that Mrs. Dela Cruz should relocate her house because it stood right on the path where everybody passed through including the *engkantos*. A few days before, one of the sons developed a high fever and then started talking to somebody the family members could not see. They suspected that he was befriended by an *engkanto* after visiting Pundang with his friends. It was fortunate that the engkantos took pity on him after they offered a live chicken, candies and cigarettes. He was supposed to have hit some being while he was cutting a tree branch in Pundang.

I was too young to remember when it happened. Myra was three years older than me, the eldest of Mana Nora's children. Myra became my best friend. We became classmates starting in Grade 2 although I did not remember her in Grade 1. I was reminded later that she stopped schooling after she contracted a mysterious skin disease which was the reason why she dressed in overalls and always wore long sleeved shirts. She had scars at the back of her hands which were very visible because she had fair skin.

One day, Myra came with us to bathe at the artesian well after we swam at the beach. It was noon. We were noisy as we took turns pumping water and hitting each other.. An elderly woman who lived nearby told us to hush because it was a holy hour for the *engkantos* but it was already too late.

When Myra came home, she noticed pink patches all over her body. Later, the patches started to itch and became blisters. Not long after, she could no longer lie down as the blisters became wounds. The doctor could not explain what inflicted Myra so the family sought different shamans from all over the island and even from neighboring towns.

They have consulted all the shamans referred to them but nothing could heal Myra's wounds until they were told about the *albularyo* from Masbate. Upon seeing Myra's condition, Mano Intoy felt that somebody was repelling his presence. He warned the family that it was a powerful *engkanto* that inflicted the wounds.

Mano Intoy performed incantations and fumigated the surroundings with incense of *kamangyan* and offered a live white chicken. After reciting the incantations, he fell to the ground unconscious. When he woke up, he asked for water and sat for a long while to recover. He dabbed some ointments to Myra's wounds made from leaves, roots and oil that he concocted himself. A few days later, the wounds started to dry.

It took several more months before the wounds completely healed and they left scars all over her body. The shaman advised them to continue applying the ointment to her scars which thankfully were only skin deep.

Myra continued to wear long sleeved shirts and overalls until the scars started to fade. She grew up to be pretty and smart but she was always delicate. The only reminder of that unfortunate event were the lingering brown spots on the back of her hands like some fading Henna tattoo.

Chapter 13: The Tragedy at Sea

It was an ordinary Sunday in January of 1985 when the MV Del Mar sailed for the town of Allen. The motor boat was filled with passengers, copra and dried *gulaman*. Some of the passengers were the graduating honors class of Capul Elementary School who were going to take the scholarship exam in Catarman. They were accompanied by their parents and some teachers.

The sea was calm when they sailed from Sangbungto, a rather unusually calm January when the eastern monsoon was still in effect that usually brings winds and rains until February.

The young students were excited and anxious at the same time with the scholarship that they will get and the upcoming graduation in March. They were in high spirits being with their friends.

As they approached Igang point near the island of San Antonio, they encountered several whirlpools that tipped the MV Del Mar to its side. The crew rushed to the opposite side of the boat and tried to balance it in place. There was a commotion and the passengers panicked. There were cries of pleadings and prayers mixed with cries for help while the whirlpools brought the passenger ship slowly sinking. Then the boat capsized, turning it upside-down. The younger passengers were the first to surface above the water while the crew members tried to save everyone within their reach. However, the strong current pushed the boat further away from the nearest island and was adrift for three days.

With the boat upside down, the passengers clung to the outrigger and whatever they could hold on to. They ate whatever they could: sea weeds, rotten fruits, banana peels and even small fishes. The older passengers were the first to give up due to the cold, fatigue and hunger. The crew members tied the dead bodies to the outriggers but the current loosen and washed some of them away. Some were never recovered.

Two of the passengers were my cousin Marielle and her mother Dada Flora. Marielle recalled that she lost hope while looking at the bodies of her friends who have died. The crew tied them to the outrigger so they would not be carried away by the current. To calm herself and to maintain her sanity, she talked to them aloud asking them to tell their families back home where exactly they were. She waved and talked to the sea gulls who were circling above them, telling them to tell her father Baba Noli that they were floating at sea. She believed that they had circled the island of Capul several times over the course of the three days but they were not spotted by the villagers because of the big waves. One time, they were very near the island and could even see people on land but people on the island could not see them. They were too exhausted to swim.

Back home, the transistor radios were open in full volume waiting for any update. Everyone in the village had a friend or relative among the passengers. The naval officers informed the neighboring islands about the tragedy and there were ongoing rescue operations scouring the sea for possible bodies.

On the third day, a fishing boat from Masbate saw them. Marielle was the first one to swim to the rescue boat but Dada Flora was too weak so she went back. Only five of them were rescued by the fishing boat. A bigger rescue boat of the Masbate Coast Guard finally rescued them near the Ticao point around five hundred nautical miles from where they capsized. The surviving passengers were brought to the hospital but unfortunately some more died while being treated.

Baba Noli called the Masbate Coast Guard upon hearing the news over DYMA. He was disheartened when he was told that no children survived the tragedy. The names of the survivors were not yet known so the families left immediately for Masbate to check on their relatives. Baba Noli was already losing hope that he had lost Marielle, his youngest, so he was overjoyed when he saw both Marielle and Dada Flora among the survivors in the hospital. Apparently, the Coast Guard did not realize that Marielle was only eleven years old because she was tall for her age.

The days and nights before the rescue was a living hell for the islanders. Almost everyone had a relative among the passengers. Some of the dead bodies were found after several days in different parts of Masbate. They were only identified by their clothes or whatever was left of their dress. Others were never recovered, forever claimed by the sea.

People did not eat fish for several weeks thinking that the dead bodies were eaten by the fishes. Others look at the sea with disdain especially those whose family members were never recovered.

One of the unrecovered casualties was Mr. Cajandab, a former teacher and member of the high school band. Another unrecovered body was that of the band guitarist.

Since the sea tragedy, people claimed to have heard the banging of the musical instruments in the band room. The town wanted to have a collective amnesia about the tragedy while the families wanted to believe that their lost family member actually survived but had amnesia so they could not come back yet.

"Somebody saw Mr. Cajandab in Cataingan, Masbate. He survived the tragedy." A neighbor was told by another neighbor that somebody saw Mr. Cajandab in the market in Masbate.

"He talked to him but he did not recognize Mana Esther. But Mana Esther was very certain that it was him, Mr. Cajandab. He did not speak and he just walked away when she asked him how he was.

The news spread like wildfire on the island. But one of the survivors attested that he saw Mr. Cajandab was among those who had died on the second day. The crew tied his body along with the others but he was washed away by the strong current. For the wife, it was what she wanted to hear all along.

Mana Clara sailed for Masbate to verify the news. She provided pictures of her husband to the Barangay Captain and asked around if anyone had seen him in the village.

"Have you seen my husband? Here he is. . ." Showing the picture of Mr. Cajandab to everyone in the village hoping that her husband survived the tragedy.

Nobody knew or had seen Mr. Cajandab but she took note that there were two women who were whispering to each other and made suspicious glances to Mana Clara while she was asking around in the fishing village in Cataingan, Masbate.

Mana Clara left with a heavy heart. Whatever hope that she had to see her husband was extinguished.

People flocked around Mana Clara when she returned to the island.

"They probably saw him but they don't want to tell you the truth." Said Mana Virgie, her saliva ejected from what remained of her teeth. Her hollow cheeks bloated while chewing on boiled camote.

"Yes, I think they were hiding a secret." Concurred Mana Sylvia, her three month old son dangling from her sides while her one year old daughter was tugging at her skirt.

"I believe one of them was the woman who took Mr. Cajandab. He probably lost his memory while floating at sea. Isn't it like in the movies when a person has no memory of his previous life? Countered Mana Nimfa the cousin of Mana Clara.

"So Mr. Cajandab has amnesia." Mana Maria said victoriously. "I heard it somewhere."

And so it was resolved by everybody that Mr. Cajandab had amnesia and he was living with another woman who did not tell him that his wife was looking for him.

A year later, another sighting of Mr, Cajandab was reported in Bantayan, Cebu.

"He was selling dried fish. He has become a fisherman and dark-complexioned. He was with a woman who was pregnant." Reported Mano Bering who was a crew of the boat selling capiz shells in Cebu.

"I talked to him in Inabaknon and he paused for a while but he did not respond. He left without saying a word. I think he knew who I was" continued Mano Bering.

Mana Clara has enlisted the help of fortune tellers and spirit questors who claimed that her husband may not be dead. With the new sightings, Mana Clara's hope was renewed and she embarked on a trip to Bantayan Island in Cebu with her youngest daughter.

"He looks familiar. I think I saw him once or twice." Claimed one market vendor.

Mana Clara's heart raced. Her faith was re-ignited that she will be reunited again with her husband.

"When did you see him? Who was with him? Are you certain that it was my husband? Mana Clara asked in succession.

"Wait, your husband is a bit short and thin. . . I think the one I saw was taller and fat." The vendor hesitated and was taken aback by Mana Clara's enthusiasm. She doesn't want to give false hope to Mana Clara.

"He may have gotten fat. Or he may have gotten dark." Mana Clara encouraged the vendor to tell her more about the man that looked like her husband.

"He usually sells dried fish during the tabu. Come back tomorrow. He comes early in the morning." Added the vendor.

Mana Clara's excitement was beyond her. It had been more than a year when the tragedy happened. He looked for clues in her dreams but her husband seldom visited her in her dreams.

The following day, Mana Clara went to the market at five o'clock in the morning feeling giddy and anxious at the same time. She went to the same stall and looked for the vendor that she talked to the previous day and waited for her husband to show up. She had been rehearsing the things she wanted to say in her mind. She dragged her daughter out of the room that she rented near the dock and took out the pictures of the family in her purse.

The vendor showed them the stall where he saw the man but another vendor had taken over the place. They waited until lunchtime but they left disappointed. The tabu vendors have left and the regular stall owners have folded back the extension awnings of their stalls but still her husband did not show up. Mana Clara came back the following day but she was disappointed again.

"Maybe the vendor warned him that you were looking for him so he did not come." Mana Virgie was almost certain about her theory.

"The vendor might be a relative of the new wife so he did not want you to see your husband." Chimed Mana Sylvia, pushing a piece of bread to her children and while the youngest child was sucking on her dangling breasts.

The saga continued. It took several years for Mana Clara and the children to finally accept that their father was dead.

Chapter 14: Gamblers and Thieves

San Luis is a small village with over a hundred houses that clustered around the narrow patch of land along the bay. On the southern part of the village is the river that goes up the farming hamlet of Ilawod and Diraya while the western part is the rice paddies and vegetable lots against the backdrop of mountain ranges that also serve as a border to the neighboring village of Aguin.

Whether we like it or not, our lives intertwine with one another. No secret remained for long. Each detail of our lives is public information shared by everyone in the village. We were known not by our names but by our mothers or fathers. The wife is known by her husband so she is called by her first name followed by the name of her husband.

There were secrets that were being openly talked about even if they involved marital relationships like the philandering husband or worse, the unfaithful wife who had an illicit affair with a younger man. The child was scrutinized from head to foot to see which parent he looked alike. Tongues wag if a girl got pregnant out of wedlock but soon forgot when a newer controversy came up.

Our house is sandwiched by two other houses between the plaza and the chapel so our street is the center of sorts of the village. There were two big stores on either corner in our front so those from the hinterlands who came to the village to buy their provisions go to our street bringing not only their produce but stories about their families near and far. Everyone was updated about the daughter who went to Manila to work as a maid, how much she sent to her family and even the names of her employers. The son who got lucky from being a stevedore in Divisoria now owns a stall. How much he earns was also a common knowledge; so he now owned a house in Cavite where he was relocated by the government along with other vendors living in the shanties in Parola district and along the estero in Sta. Cruz.

Card games were one of the diversions of the well-to-dos or those who can afford not to till their own land as well as those who receive monthly support from their children in Manila. The store on our right corner was busy not only with their brisk business but with card game enthusiasts from around the town and the other villages especially on weekends.

Laughter and hooting would be heard every now and then from the gamblers. One voice could be easily distinguished from the rest, a woman whose laughter was five-note, the first three were the same with the fourth rising abruptly and the last the highest note, louder and sustained. Hers was the loudest laugh especially when she hit the *"todas"*.

Nanay's hands were always full with housework. If she was not busy cooking, she was working on the farm with Tatay. The winners from the card games usually treated the other players with cassava balls or banana fritters so we hung the basket of delicacies in our front window for everyone to see.

"Gambling is never good. Nor any vices. Drinking is okay when done occasionally." Nanay warned me regularly. "Gamblers are indolent people who depend their luck on the cards. When you work for a living, you are sure to eat. I will not allow any of you to learn gambling of any form. That is never good."

The village was peaceful and there were hardly any crimes reported except for petty theft. "Those who steal are indolent. Instead of working, they steal other people's crops." Nanay shook her head upon discovering that the banana that was almost ripe was stolen.

Chapter 15: The Weaver

During off-farming seasons, Nanay wove *tipo* or mats and baskets from *pandan* and *buri* leaves that grew abundantly around the farm house. The mats from *pandan* are used for sleeping while those made from *buri* are used for drying rice or corn. Nanay also made *bi-ul* or large rice storage baskets or *bakag*, the smaller one.

To make mats, she harvested the mature leaves, removed the thorns, cut them into strips then rolled them into discs and dried them in the sun. The dried strips are hung overnight on the awning of the house to straighten them and to soften the fibers before they are uniformly cut into strips. I would watch Nanay weave in the living room well into the night while she tells me stories or *surusurumaton*. Nanay sold the mats and baskets to our neighbors. Sometimes, visiting relatives from Manila would order the mats as *pasalubong*. "They love the *tipo* because it is cool unlike the *kutson*." They would say. Until now, I have had this dream of lying beside Nanay, the scent of the new mats lingering in my nose.

Perhaps one of my favorite stories of Nanay was of a fairy that married an ordinary mortal and produced beautiful children. The story go on like this:

> One day, a young farmer saw the fairies bathing in the river. He was mesmerized by their ethereal beauty and he fell in love with one of them. At night, he could not sleep thinking about how beautiful the fairy was so every day, he waited for them to come and soon, he discovered where they hung their wings. Since then, he dreamt of the lovely fairy day and night and wanted to talk to her so he devised a plan.
>
> While the fairies were enjoying themselves bathing in the crystal clear river, he took her wings and hid it in the pit that he covered with soil. Soon, the fairies retrieved their wings leaving behind

the other one because she could not find her own. The young man approached her and pretended to help her look for her wings.

Because they could not locate her wings, she agreed to go home with him and later on they married and had four children. She resigned to her fate and forgot about her wings and her enchanted life. Her husband loved her very much and he provided for her every need so she was happy and content.

One day, the children were playing in the backyard when they accidentally unearthed her wings. She took it and went home to her kingdom leaving her family behind. Grief-stricken, the husband became ill and forgot his responsibility to his children. One day, he announced that he will embark on a journey to search for his wife. He went far and wide to look for her but he was unsuccessful.

Finally, he saw the fairies again bathing in the river but they hurriedly left when they saw him. He attempted to run after them but they quickly disappeared. He searched day and night until finally he discovered their hidden kingdom. He went to the king and begged him for his wife. The king took pity on him but he put him to a test by asking him to identify his wife from among the lovely fairies.

"But they all looked the same!" he protested and he could not identify his wife. Apparently, his wife had forgotten her life with him and their children. Finally, he asked the king if he could hold their hands and the king agreed. He was able to identify his wife because she had needle pricks on her hands. She sewed her children's clothes herself. When he held her hands, she instantly remembered who he was and agreed to go with him. The fairies bid them goodbye and they left the kingdom to go home. It only took them a while to be home with their children who were overjoyed when they saw their parents.

Sometimes, she put on her wings and took her children to different places. But she did not think of going away again because she was content with her life with her family.

Chapter 16: Harvest Season

Nanay cut a few stalks of rice, the best grains and put them on the dike. "It's for the birds," she said. "Also for the spirits of our ancestors who had tilled the same soil".

She performed the Novena of the Glorious Mystery and thanked the heavens for the harvest, good or bad.

Three days later, the golden yellow grains were ready for harvest. Garbed with a long sleeve garment worn over a shirt and *buri* hat, we harvested the grains with a scythe. The harvesters move in unison, grabbing the stalks with their left, the scythe in their right, they swiftly cut the stalks and lay on the dike. Later on the stalks and carried to the barn where it will be threshed manually by trampling it over with feet. Then the grains are threshed or winnowed to separate the good grains from empty husks. Finally, the grains are dried under the sun for at least two days before they are stored in sacks or *bi-ul*.

The harvest season is the best time of the year; farmers pay the businessmen with grains for the pesticides and fertilizers. Rice was also bartered for fish and other household needs.

During this time, we stayed in Baquiw since it was also vacation time from school. Aside from the small hut on the hill near the paddies, Tatay and my brothers also constructed a barn where we threshed and stored the rice.

Pounding rice was not my favorite task but because there was no rice mill in the village yet, my siblings and I took turns with the wooden pestle and mortar.

Harvest time also meant that the food vendors would come with their freshly cooked rice cakes and dried fish which we bartered with rice. Every afternoon, I would wait for Dada Marla with her *puto ligong* still warm from the steamer. Her *puto ligong* was soft and had the aroma of fresh coconut wine that she used to ferment the ground rice.

The end of the harvest was celebrated with a dance at the barn. My uncle who lived nearby would bring his *radyopuno* while the farmers drunk and danced till the wee hours. We, the children had *pinipilig* made from the unripe rice in the fields.

We would stay in Baquiw for the rest of the summer and only returned to the village before the opening of the classes. While there, Nanay would cook delicacies like *mikin*, banana fritters and coconut-stuffed cassava balls that I sell during Sundays at the cockfight in Sitio Bel-at. One time, the cops came in the middle of the cockfight and arrested the men since it was illegal. Seeing the gamblers scamper in every direction, I also ran and hid at the back of one of the houses although I was not pursued by the police.

Although I love the farm, I dreaded the nights because it was too dark. The animals and insects in the meadows would outdo each other with their sounds and hooting. I imagined them arguing to each other who will be the first to attack us and eat us alive. Before midnight, the *kikik* and *kakak* would hover around the house so I would hide under the blanket until I would fall asleep.

Our farm house was rather small, consisting of one room where everybody slept and a small kitchen and fireplace directly facing the main door and a small porch which was also used as sleeping quarters. We had no toilet just like other houses during the time. We got our drinking water from a spring one hundred meters uphill where our nearest neighbor lived. The other neighbor lived on the foot of the adjacent hill and when our elders called each other, they would shout and talk loudly like they were beside each other. I guess that is why we have big voices.

Chapter 17: Graduation from Elementary

The day of my grade school graduation came. Looking stuffed in my outfit of oversize white shirt borrowed from a relative and my new black pants big enough until my fourteenth birthday I walked awkwardly in my new leather shoes that were also big for my skinny feet. Nanay stuffed my toes with extra cloth so my shoes could fit, which was a gift from my oldest brother. When I took the podium for my valedictory address, I remembered the very first time that I stood on that rectangular stage decorated with woven coconut fronds and bedecked with paper roses and *Kalachuche* blooms. I looked far away into the horizon. It was a perfect summer day.

The sun was setting while I said:

"Today, I thank my parents for their commitment to education by sending me to school. Secondly, I thank my teachers for the valuable lessons that will become the foundation of my lifelong education."

"This is only the first step of our academic journey" I remember saying while the sun was setting and turned luminous in the horizon. I was looking out to the sea and imagined what lies beyond the cloak of islands covering the mouth of the San Bernardino Strait.

That night, we had a simple feast consisting of fried fish and chicken stewed in coconut milk, a graduation gift from my godparents.

I was one of the top students in the admission exam at the Capul Agro & Industrial School. I belonged to the first section, the honors class for boys while my cousin Myra was in Section 2, the honors class for the girls. By our second year, the honors class for boys and girls were combined and the other two sections were determined based on their academic grades.

Elsa accompanied me to school during the enrolment and oriented me about where my rooms were although I have been to the campus before when I attended the graduation of Daria and Mano Boyet.

CAIS is one of the two high schools on the island. The other one was located in Barangay Landusan on the western part of the island where the students from the neighboring villages enrolled.

Every Sunday afternoon, I and Elsa walked the six kilometer sandy road to the poblacion and returned after our last class on Friday afternoons. Every week I carried the straw basket with our provision for the week consisting of one *ganta* of rice, coconut, dried fish and vegetables that we harvested from the farm. On some occasions, we leave at dawn on Mondays with our torch made of dried twigs to scare-off the dogs and other harmful animals along the way. Most of the time, we were with other students so it was not much of a chore.

I quickly made friends with my new classmates and excelled in classes that include subjects in Agriculture and Farm Mechanics. But I dreaded Mathematics. I love literature and the arts and I love to read. Soon I discovered the short stories of NVM Gonzales, Nick Joaquin, Carlos Bulusan and Paz Marquez Benitez who became my favorite authors.

I was not a diligent student and I got bored reading my notes. When the teacher was discussing the lessons, I listened attentively and understood the terms then wrote short notes which I reviewed before the exam. I love recitations so even if I don't get perfect scores in the periodical exams, they compensate for my grades.

High school introduced me to betamax houses. During this time, the town had electricity from six o'clock to around ten o'clock but we still used kerosene lamps at Tata Bala's which often go out a little after suppertime. The betamax houses offered two shows per night consisting of taped musical programs and Tagalog movies of different genres. My favorites were the dramas and fantasies featuring my favorite love teams from That's Entertainment.

It was an magical experience for me watching television shows for the first time. I read about the TV and movie industry in the tabloids that was used as a wrapper for the dried fish that Tatay bought when he sold copra in Matnog. I also heard about the artistas in radio so I was overjoyed when I finally saw them in the movies. In fact, I heard about the death of Julie Vega, a very famous teen actress, on the radio and how the announcers became very emotional while describing the movies that she made when she was alive and the TV shows that she starred in. I saw her movies finally when she was already dead.

My favorite actresses were Sharon Cuneta and Maricel Soriano among others. I also liked the petite singer-actress Manilyn Reynes especially when she sang with Janno Gibbs on That's entertainment together with other young talents.

The entrance fee for the betamax show was P2.00 which was also the fare for the motorcycle ride from San Luis to the town so Elsa and I would choose to walk even if we were given fare money in order to be able to watch the show. Oh how I despised Cherie Gil when she maltreated Sharon Cuneta in "Bituing Walang Ningning" and cheered when Sharon eventually emerged victorious at the end of the story. I love stories of survival and eventual success such as "Pasan Ko ang Daigdig" where Sharon played a young singer from the slums who became famous.

The show the previous night would be the talk of the campus the following day in between classes. The girls would talk about the drama show while the boys love the *bakbakan* or action movies.

I have never left the island during this time unlike my other classmates who have gone to Manila so I did not have any idea about what was happening outside of the island.

Chapter 18: The Second Storm

Elsa was always sickly even as a child. Nanay recalled that when she was pregnant, she could feel some elementals hovering around her or inside the house while waiting for her to give birth. "Just like with Ella", she recalled. She could hear voices deep at night or smell something which was not of human source. Elsa was born on a rainy day in the third week of January when the leaves of the rice started to turn darker green. The weeds needed to be uprooted in the paddies lest they overtake the plants and compete for the nutrients of the soil. She was tall and slender but with a weak cry. The *partira* cautioned Nanay not to take her out of the house without saying The Lord's Prayer. Elsa was baptized with the name Lotty to confuse the *engkantos* about her and she was guarded by the older sisters while growing up. She was called by her baptismal name in school.

Elsa grew up to be tall for her age. She towers above her classmates during her elementary graduation wherein she was the valedictorian. Actually, she was the consistent valedictorian since grade one, excelling in every subject except Physical Education due to her asthma.

During planting and harvest seasons, Elsa was tasked to cook our meals and she was only given lighter tasks because she tires fast. While weeding the vegetable patch, she would be assigned near the shade.

Being pretty, she had a few suitors who wanted to visit her at home but she would not entertain them. In fact, she never had a boyfriend and she did not intend to have one until she finished college.

"I want to become a teacher. I want to be the first teacher in the family." Elsa declared while we were walking to town one Sunday afternoon.

"I want to be a radio announcer." I said tentatively.

"I will support your studies when I become a teacher. We don't expect anyone to help us because our older siblings have families of their own." She added.

"That is true. They have not responded to my letter asking for a new pair of shoes for the next school year." I said looking at my worn-out slippers.

We were optimistic about our plans and we talked about it often. "We will become successful." We were sure about it.

A motorcycle wheeled past us and left a column of dust and smoke so we paused for a while. Elsa coughed so hard so we rested awhile by the shade and only proceeded when Elsa had steadied herself. We reached the municipal cemetery at dusk which was just perfect so that people would not stare at us as we passed by. Tata Bala's house was still around five hundred meters and Elsa does not want to be seen by her classmates walking in town.

In February of her junior year, Elsa was selected as one of the Corps Sponsor during the Tactical Inspection for the Citizen's Army Training along with other pretty girls in the campus. She was assigned to the tallest officer because she dwarfed the other boys. A few days before the Tactical Inspection, she suddenly fell while walking with her classmates so she was rushed to the hospital. Determined as she was, she felt better and was able to parade with the other girls on the day of the tactical inspection. Later on, her picture with the other girls is the only surviving picture of her because the others were washed out by the different typhoons that battered our house.

I was the second honors during my freshman year while Elsa was third honors for the juniors at the end of that school year. Neither Nanay nor Tatay attended the recognition ceremony so we just accepted our certificates by ourselves.

In her senior year, Elsa was able to attend the first grading exam although she had been going in and out of the hospital more often so we took motorcycle rides in going to town.

One day, she fell down while alighting from the motorcycle in front of the house of Tata Bala. I helped her out as she anxiously looked around if any of her classmates witnessed the incident. I knew that she was really sick after that but she did not want to burden anyone with her illness. At this time, I was not informed about her condition nor the seriousness of her illness.

"I want to be a teacher so I can help our parents so they can rest from farming". Elsa repeated while I was braiding her long hair one afternoon before we went to class. I noticed that she had some lice so I dusted them off her hair.

Two days after, she fell again while climbing the stairs going to the Vocational Agriculture Building so she was rushed by her classmates to the hospital. It was after the first periodical exams and they were rehearsing for the calisthenics for the upcoming town fiesta at the end of July.

Elsa stayed the following week in the hospital while she underwent different tests. She looked tired and pale. The doctor asked us for blood donors from among our relatives and the transfusion was immediate.

We stayed at the hospital until the end of July. I peeked from her window while my classmates swayed to the marching band with their colorful costumes representing the different Philippine tribes. I helped her to the chair by the window so she could also witness the parade going by. As I helped her stand up, I noticed the blood clots in her arms.

Nanay and Tatay took turns accompanying her in the hospital while I took a watch after my classes and she would ask me to update her about the goings on in the campus. Nanay made her eat *ensaladang ampalaya* for her blood circulation to improve and Elsa swallowed them reluctantly even if she wanted to vomit them out. I ate some to encourage her to eat more but she had no appetite.

The doctors did not allow her to go back to school so we brought her home with her medicines. Even with her condition, she was hopeful that she would get better in time. We would talk about our plans, her plans when she gets back to school and when she graduates from college. She did not realize that she had a terminal illness and she was awaiting death. No one in the family talked about it.

When the grades for the first grading were posted, Elsa was number four in the honor list. Her classmates wanted to visit her at home but she would not hear of it. She didn't want to be seen in her condition, especially by her friends. She was becoming more and more dependent on Nanay. She could not get up on her own or bathe on her own. On Friday nights, she would anticipate my return, propped with pillows on her back, waiting for my stories of the events in school. She would ask about her classmates, her teachers and everything that happened during the week. She missed school.

Before she was discharged from the district hospital, the doctors advised us to bring her to a bigger hospital in Calbayog City while waiting for her laboratory results that were sent to the Provincial Hospital. On the day that the results were sent back, I saw Nanay and Tatay talking in whispers looking disappointed and defeated. Even at this point, I was not told that Elsa's condition was a terminal case.

The day of the trip to Calbayog City came so I woke up early to see her go.

"Nay, why are you not preparing for the trip yet? Aren't you leaving for Calbayog"

Nanay did not respond and looked away. She was cooking breakfast and washing the dishes, pretending that she did not hear me. She continued with what she was doing.

I thought that they were postponing the trip until we had enough money but I did not suspect that they were not leaving anytime soon. It was only later that I learned that the doctor had talked to them that Elsa had stage 4 leukemia. It was too late and only a miracle could save her. I remembered the blood clots on her arms after her transfusion. The blood was no longer accepted by her system.

They say that there are days and events in life that you will remember vividly like they happened only yesterday. For me, September 13, 1988 was one of those. The night before was the victory ball of the sports fest so there was a dance at the school grounds. It was a Friday and I intended to go home the following morning. During this time I was staying with Daria in her house in Zone Liang and she had given birth to her eldest son. While my classmates were enjoying the dance, I felt that something was not right. I was anxious and ominous about an impending tragedy. I stayed away from the dance floor but her classmates saw me and dragged me to dance so I reluctantly obliged. That night, I barely slept and dreamt of something vague and incomprehensible that I woke up at dawn, earlier than usual. Something was not right.

On the way to my cousin's house, I saw another cousin and a neighbor at the hardware store who casually told me that Elsa had passed on. They were buying wood and nails for the coffin.

I felt lightheaded and my mind shut off but I continued walking. My cousins already knew the news and in fact was waiting for me as I was riding with them home.

I refused to believe that Elsa was gone so I didn't see her at once. I ran to my parents' room and cried silently. People called and asked if I wanted to eat but I ignored them. I was in that state when I heard a powerful male voice saying:

"Elsa is in a better place now so you have to accept that she's gone. She's no longer in pain and she's happy." I was instantly calmed and decided to see Elsa on her deathbed. I would remember that voice vividly for the rest of my life. It was firm but reassuring. It was a unique voice that I have never heard so I knew it was God talking to me.

I composed myself and went to see her lying in state in the folding bed where she died. Nanay dressed her in her white and pink school uniform. She looked peaceful and I thought that she had a faint smile on her lips. I combed her long black hair like I used to.

Elsa died at day break while Nanay was trying to give her her medicines. She was gasping for breath and was terrified because knew she was dying. Nanay propped some pillows on her back and calmed her. Elsa relaxed and slept after taking her medicines. She never woke up again.

When Elsa was in the hospital, Dada Iding dreamt of her in a wedding dress. She was walking on a mist and at the end of the aisle was a faceless man receiving her in her splendid dress. She asked her to sew her that dress.

Her classmates and teachers came along with our relatives upon learning of the news. She was buried the following day near the grave of Ella but we learned that Ella's grave was one of those that were accidentally dug when a mausoleum was built by the rich family when their matriarch was buried. Her grave was marked by a wooden cross that bears her baptismal name, birthday and date of death.

Nanay was unconsolable. I wanted to embrace her but I did not know what to say. While this was happening, I was stuck in my feet from a distance watching them bury her. Several days later, I dreamt of being the one buried and I woke up sweating and convalescing from high fever.

I did not go home for two weeks after the burial. I could not face the thought that Elsa would not be in her bed by the living room when I returned. After Elsa died, the house felt empty and quiet. I would look at every corner of the house expecting that she would materialize, healthier and livelier than the last time I saw.

On the third night after her death, she visited me in my dream. We met every night from then until the 40th day of her passing. She looked pretty and healthy. We would talk about anything like we used to. Oftentimes, we picked up from where we were and at dawn, she would bid farewell and I would plead with her to stay. I would wake up crying.

My family was worried as I got so thin and ghastly. I lost my appetite.

"Your souls are intertwined so you need to be separated." People remarked.

Her death made me a man at fourteen. On the other hand, Dong had taken the responsibility of helping Tatay in the farm full time after his high school graduation. Mano Boyet left for Manila the summer after his high school graduation and he actually returned home upon learning that Elsa had died. He arrived the week after her burial and stayed a couple of months before leaving again. My other siblings did not make it home and it was still years after we'd see them again.

I visited a shaman for nine consecutive Fridays who performed a ritual. He wrote some prayers on a piece of paper, burned it and then made me drink the water containing its ashes. Sometimes, the ashes would gag me but I need to swallow it as part of the ritual. My dreams about

Elsa continued. She still came every night and we talked until I woke up calling her name bidding her not to go.

Elsa also visited me in my waking hours.

Classes were suspended that day because of a typhoon. When it was time to cook our lunch Daria asked me to buy some condiments in the nearby store. It was raining and the wind was blowing hard from the ocean so I was drenched when I returned from the kitchen door. I pushed the door but it was stuck, the jambs swelling from rain water. I was putting down my umbrella when the door opened from inside. From the split bamboo, I could see a girl wearing a white blouse and pink skirt.

"Was it you who opened the door?" Daria was folding the baby's clothes in the living room.

"No, I have not gotten up since you left."

I did not want Daria to be scared so I said nothing further. When I told her about it later, she believed it was Elsa who opened the door for me.

Two nights after that first incident, I was reviewing for my exam with only the kerosene lamp. There was still no electricity due to the typhoon. I was reading my notes in the day bed when I fell asleep. Suddenly, I was roused by the banging of the pots in the kitchen. The lamp had started licking the wall paper when I woke up so I frantically moved the lamp away from the partition. When I checked the kitchen, the lid of the pot where we put our leftover food was open.

"What was that noise?" Daria woke up and went downstairs.

"The house almost burned if I did not wake up with the banging of the pot." I showed her the blackened partition and the lid of the pot on the kitchen table.

"Maybe the cat did it." Daria said nonchalantly. We did not discuss it further and I went upstairs but I was not able to sleep at once thinking that Elsa had roused me from my sleep and saved all of us.

"I want to become a radio announcer so I will be taking up Mass Communications in College" I and Levi were walking to town on a Sunday afternoon one month before my high school graduation. It took us one hour on foot along the six kilometer feeder road to the poblacion.

"I might go to Manila after our high school graduation. My parents could not afford to send me to college." Levi was a bit sad with the thought.

"Well, I might not be going to college too. Unless I get that scholarship from UP. In that case, I might go to Manila too and become a working student". That was my plan. I would finish college no matter what. The responsibility rests on my shoulders now.

"That will be exciting!" "We will still see each other in Manila and maybe go out on our days off." Levi's mood lighted up again.

"That's the plan. Then we will go home together on fiestas!"

"Yes! We will never part" I assured Levi again.

A ripe guava by the roadside caught our attention. We ventured further away from the roadside to check the other trees and much on them right away.

"Look up! There's also *lamon-lamon*!" I looked up to see a roof of yellow-orange marbles on the vines. We harvested all the ripe fruits that we could and left a trail of peels and seeds along the way. Before we knew it, we were approaching the public cemetery at the edge of the town.

"Esperanza Salazar. Mario Magdaraog. Clara Dela Vega. Santos Cabili." We read aloud the tombstones as we passed along then dashed to the gate of the Central School while giggling with our bags of rice and vegetables for the week. We were scared that the souls of the dead would come along with us so we hurried while we laughed at our childish antics.

Levi also lived with us at Tata Bala's house for some time along with another friend Betto.

There were days when we did not have something to eat so the fruits around Tata Bala's house were a big help. The generous breadfruit saved us on some days when we had nothing but rice. If we had money to buy sugar, it was already a feast and one big fruit would last us until the following day. Some days I go to school with my stomach empty but it did not discourage me a bit. I was determined to reach my goals.

Near the entrance of Sitio Marasbaras was a rocky cliff with stunted century-old trees growing among the limestone as if keeping guard of the place. At night, their sinister shadows looked like demons waiting to gorge a child so we avoided going home very late so we could pass by the cliff while it was still light. The air always felt colder on this part even during hot days which made our hairs stand up.

"Please let us pass by", we murmured as we passed along, ever careful not to disturb the *engkantos* dwelling in the place. Everyone was quiet while passing by the cliff and then we would dash to the first houses along the road.

One afternoon, there was a commotion at school.

"Mano Renato, the father of Carla had an accident while traversing the dirt road near the rocky cliffs in Marasbaras." Our English teacher announced with shock. Mano Renato's family owned a store where I buy school supplies. His daughter was a freshman.

The accident happened in broad daylight. The driver sustained broken limbs and a skull like it was hit by a hard object but his motorcycle only needed minor repairs. Mano

Simon, the lone passenger sustained minor injuries and was more shocked by what happened to the driver than with the impact of the accident. It was lunchtime and they were speeding by the cliff when they hit a protruding rock and they skidded to the ground. Blood was spilled on the sandy road.

Mano Renato's lifeless body was brought to the hospital which was a stone's throw away from the campus. Carla ran to the hospital upon hearing the news bawling followed by some of her classmates. I knew Mano Renato personally because I rode with him on the few times that I had spare money for the motorcycle fare. I remembered his ready smile and jovial personality and murmured some prayers.

Mano Renato was not the first, nor the last driver who met the same fate in almost the same exact spot where family members would light some candles in a wooden cross erected as a sort of memorial and warning. That Friday afternoon, everyone was quiet as we passed by noting the caked blood on the stones. We crossed ourselves as we walked past the spot.

"I believe they hit something that belonged to the engkanto." Jerry, an upperclassman said. Everyone agreed.

When a person dies due to an accident or a sickness caused by *engkantos*, they will travel to the other realm. They lived in the place where they died together with the *engkantos*.

It was a tradition during Holy Week for our family to attend the religious activities in the Poblacion and we would walk together with the other families on Holy Thursday. On one occasion, a toddler was crying while pointing at the "store" in the cliff asking for candy. The child was only pacified after her father bought her some candy in the next village of Cantil.

Chapter 19: The Engkantos

Tata Bala's house had a spacious yard. The front yard was planted with Bermuda grass where we lied down to read or simply chat, especially on moonlit nights. Because of the canopy of the fruit trees around the house, the place looked dark with ominous shadows at night. Sometimes, we would talk in the dark when the kerosene lamp goes out at night to save gas. Sometimes, we sleep early or giggle in the dark if we run out of kerosene.

The house was made of wood and bamboo with thatch walls and roof. The floor in the main house was raised from the ground to accommodate the chicken coops and duck pens below. Their crowing and quacking woke us up every day at dawn so Tata Bala rose very early to feed them. The wooden stairs leading to the main house had bamboo railings that I slid down when I was little. The doors and windows were also made of bamboo and thatch that you have to push open with a bamboo pole. The same bamboo pole is used to lock the window by sliding it crosswise against the frame. It was typical of the old houses in the province. The kitchen, which was lower than the main house, had a long wooden table and two long wooden benches on either side. The antiques and china wares were secured in a wooden chest on one side. Drinking water was drawn from earthen jars which was a natural way of keeping the water cool. One jar was used to store drinking water and another jar for washing the utensils. Tata Bala used earthen jars or pakat-tan in cooking rice. The pot made the rice smoky and sweet. Even the *paksiw* was more delicious when cooked in the *pakat-tan*.

One portion of the front yard facing the street was rented out by a newlywed couple and opened a variety store. Mana Martha, the mother-in-law, took care of the newborn baby while the couple tended the store.

"The moon was high when I went out last night. When I started walking home, I noticed that the streets were unfamiliar. Everywhere I looked, I saw tall buildings with dazzling lights. I was in another place. I was terrified!" Mana Martha was shaking while sharing her experience the previous night to some neighbors.

"I continued walking but I didn't know my way. Then I made a sign of the cross and murmured "Hesus Maria Joseph". I started praying the Lord's Prayer but I keep forgetting the lines. In the middle of my prayer, the tall buildings disappeared in an instant. When I looked around, I found myself in the corner of our street." Mana Martha was tearing while narrating her strange experience.

The people believed Mana Martha has travelled to the other realm and reminded everyone to be mindful of those around them as we live in the same space with the other beings that we do not see. They talked about it for a long time.

People believed that we co-existed with the *engkantos*. The clairvoyant people including the *tambalan* could see them. They were fair and good looking but one could identify them because they did not have a philtrum or the line between the nose and the lips. Some were friendly who would gift their host with precious gems. Others were naughty and would tinker with the household things while others would harm people by causing mysterious skin diseases, stomach ache or dysentery. Some deaths in the island were believed to be caused by these *engkantos*. To appease them, one should give them an offering, usually a live chicken, eggs, candies, cigarettes or whatever it was that the *engkantos* fancied.

Tata Bala was a *tambalan* who performed *pabawi* to take back one's spirit believed to be possessed by the *engkantos*. He used fragrant herbs like *kamangyan* to fumigate the house while chanting ancient prayers to appease the spirits.

Other than healing rituals, Tata Bala could heal common illnesses like cough, colds or flu. He would feel the person's pulse and then prescribe the medicinal plants to cure his ailment. On Tuesday and Fridays, he collected leaves, twigs, roots and barks that he hung to dry in a shed in the backyard. He put them on empty wine bottles and poured homemade coconut oil. Although it had a foul smell, the *banyos* was effective for stomach ache, headache and insect or animal bites.

Tata Bala had a mystical being for a friend who guided him while performing healing rituals for those plagued by mysterious diseases. Other than his healing powers, Tata Bala was clairvoyant so he knew who among us stole something. He had an old wooden trunk where he put his valuables like land titles, silverwares and Sunday dresses for which he kept the key on his waist along with the key of the wooden chest in the kitchen where the china wares were kept.

Tata Bala died when I was in third year high school. One day, he did not get up early in the morning; that was his routine. When I checked on him, he had chills so I fetched Dada Iding who lived in the next street and we brought him to the hospital. He did not stay long in the hospital and we brought him to Dada Aying's house, a couple of streets from Dada Iding's. He died not long after at the ripe age of 92.

When a person of "special powers" dies, they choose from among their family members to whom they would bequeath their powers. Before Tata Bala breathed his last, he called on my cousin to bequeath his powers but my cousin was scared. It was believed that one must sacrifice a family member in order to attain great powers as *tambalan*. Nanay said she would have accepted it.

One day, Mila refused to dress for school for no reason. It was the first day after the fiesta where she paraded around the town as the band majorette.

"She does not want to eat. She doesn't talk." Dada Aying cried worried about her youngest daughter. It had been two days since Mila did not get up from her bed.

"Dr. Lapuz could not identify what ails Mila so we are fetching a shaman from Masbate." It was the same tambalan who healed Myra. He had been summoned to the island several times before this.

Mila was frightened when she saw the shaman.

"Go away! Go away! You are a demon!" Mila mistook him for the *engkanto*. It was the first time that she talked since being ill. She was hysterical which attracted the neighbors who started to gather in front of the house.

"The *engkanto* could not get near her because she carries a rosary. This *engkanto* is smitten with her beauty and he wanted to marry her." The shaman was preparing his things as he just arrived. He muttered some incantation that sent Mila shaking in the corner. She calmed down afterwards and fell asleep.

The engkanto fell in love with Mila but he only admired her from afar. Later on, this *engkanto* visited her at home and Mila saw him in all the places of the house even in the bathroom.

A commotion ensued after Mila became feverish and started to attack anyone in the house including the *tambalan*. Her voice became hoarse from all the shouting even sounding like a man's. The *tambalan* struggled while four men pinned Mila on her hands and feet. The next days were intervals of frenzy and peaceful slumber with Mila begging for water when she woke up. The tambalan installed charms and other trinkets around the house and on the fourth day, Mila woke up peacefully, asked for breakfast and prepared for school.

"The *engkanto* promised not to bother Mila again for as long as she does not entertain any suitors until her eighteenth birthday. She will not marry until she is twenty one." The shaman instructed Dada Aying not to remove the things that he installed around the house and to follow the truce.

"Mila, you cannot go to school yet because you have been absent for more than two months." Dada Aying consoled Mila.

"But I went to school yesterday!" Mila was puzzled.

"You were sick. Maybe you did not remember but you were absent for so long. You will enroll again next school year."

Mila did not remember anything about the episodes of her sickness. She went back to her normal life with her parents strictly monitoring her activities. She just turned sixteen and her parents took note of the instructions of the shaman. She had admirers in school but she was not allowed to entertain anyone.

After her high school graduation, Mila went to Manila to visit her sisters and worked as a sales lady in the department store. Come July, she returned for the town fiesta. It was when she met Alberto, the son of a rich family in Capul who was one of her admirers back in high school. They fell in love and soon Alberto's family formally ask her hand in marriage and the wedding was set.

"Mila started laughing for no reason. She laughed out loud while dining with her in-laws. She also talks to herself and to an invisible person" Miriam, her niece said. She had been living with Alberto during this time. She would sneak out the house at any time of the day or night so she

I saw her one time roaming around the town, dragging her bike while Miriam walked a few steps behind her. She did not attack anyone and just laughed or talked to people. The wedding was called off. They forgot one thing: Mila just turned nineteen that summer, two years short of the marrying age.

The same shaman was summoned. Mila now stayed in her room with wooden bars to keep her from roaming around the town. Dada Aying patiently cared for her while the shaman performed rituals to repel the bad spirits. The house was cordoned off with things that will keep the engkanto from getting near Mila. After more than one month, Mila woke up perplexed about the wooden bars in her room as well as the chaos in the house.

Mila and Dada Aying travelled to Manila and stayed with her older sisters. After a few years, she married and bore two beautiful sons.

Chapter 20: The Drought

The rains stopped in February. It was the hottest time that the people remembered. The rice paddies were parched due to lack of rains. March came and the sun shone brighter every day. People looked for signs in the sky but the clouds were as luminous as cotton spread thinly on the turquoise sky.

"The sweet potato yields very small roots and the coconut trees have smaller fruits too. How are we going to survive in this kind of weather?" Tatay was shaking his head while putting his load of sweet potato on the kitchen table. The cassava had been depleted and the yams were still too small for harvest.

Nanay peeled the sweet potatoes and cooked them mixed with rice to stretch our food supply.

Each of us seven children got our share of two dried fish each. If not for the sweet potato, the bland rice would not make for a palatable fare. On other days, we had boiled plantains for breakfast and porridge for supper. Tatay and my brothers were given the biggest share because of their work on the farm. The river and water wells in the village dried up.

People took to the forest looking for *ba-ay* and *ad'dut* and other wild yam until the slopes were over-farmed too. People were even looting other farms.

The villagers prayed for rain but the sun shone brighter each day and the drought continued until the month of May. Because of this, the village council decided not to hold the fiesta because people had nothing to prepare.

"We cannot postpone the fiesta because it is the day of our patron saint. But because of the hard times, we will only have a mass on the feast day but no dancing, no cockfights and no games. The Barangay has no more funds because we used it to purchase additional pipes for the water system." The Barangay Captain announced during the meeting at the plaza.

The council agreed and the people murmured in agreement. The rice granaries are dwindling and the crops have very little yield.

"We will bathe the saints and pray for rain." Mana Quilin, the cantora suggested.

"Yes, we will make processions around the barrio. Everyone should take part." Mana Nimfa agreed. The image of the Virgin and the San Isidro were paraded around the village and was received by different families after the procession. People fervently prayed but the first week ended with no signs of rain. People were desperate.

One day on the second week of the religious processions, people woke up to cries of astonishment.

"Fish! There are plenty of fishes! Get up everyone!"

"What do you mean, fish?"

"Get out to the sea. Get your nets ready!"

"Come out everyone! Go to the sea!"

"*Salay-salay! Salay-salay!* The bay is circled by *salay-salay*"

Schools of yellowtail scud swarmed the bay. The people congregate at the bay to see the fishermen with net-full of yellowtail scud wriggling in the nets. The fishes were squirming and jumping even at the shallow parts of the bay so that we could catch them with our bare hands. People helped themselves and filled their own baskets. There was pandemonium of triumphant shouts thanking the Virgin.

"This is the gift of De Salvacion! Let us thank our Patron!" cried Mana Quilin.

"Thank you De Salvacion! You are faithful to your people!" cried Mana Nimfa while getting her share.

"More fishes in the river! Set up your traps!" Mano Winnie excitedly went home to get his nets after checking his crab traps.

"Thank you De Salvacion! You heard our prayers!"

The same phenomenon greeted the villagers for three consecutive days one week prior to the feast day. The shoreline was lined with fish drying in the sun. On the fourth day, there were dark clouds and thunderstorms. Heavy rains poured and the people rejoiced in the streets.

The fiesta was celebrated although it was not as extravagant as the previous years but there was a new and renewed hope in the way people greeted each other in the chapel during the mass. Cheers erupted after the end of the mass as Father Poten announced the miracle that happened to the faithful people of De Salvacion. People talked about it for days on end and vowed and they saw a lady at the mouth of the bay driving the fishes to the nets. Soon after the fiesta, the farmers planted the seeds in time for the next season.

Chapter 21: The Enchanted Island

From the top of the hill, the islands on the other side of the San Bernardino Straight looked like Chinese painting with different hues of blue and pastel green. Sailors passing by the strait at night claim that our island town is as mystical as the vanishing island in the middle of the strait. Instead of a sleepy, agricultural town, sailors saw a thriving city with bright lights and skyscrapers. Beautiful nymphs waved from the ports to lure the captain and spend the night at the moors only to find themselves fooled by their own eyes as their ships hit rock bottom and they were stranded for several days.

In the summer of my tenth birthday, a passenger ship ran aground in Sitio Bel-at. We were gathering shells and crabs at low tide at the marsh when we heard a commotion from the passing ship. The ship tilted to one side and eventually stopped. It was only about one hundred meters away from where the waves broke so we saw how the passengers panicked, wore their orange life jackets and prepared to jump ship. We ran home because we thought that they were pirates wanting to abduct us. At this time, there were rumors around the town that mysterious people were roaming the island to kidnap small children, slide them in sacks and bring them to faraway places as human sacrifice for newly-constructed bridges. We ran as fast as we could to tell our elders about what we saw. When we returned, people were crowded on the seashore. Some villagers launched their fishing boats to ogle at the passengers who were calmed down eventually when the boat did not sink.

One account claimed that the captain saw a beautiful lady waving from the rocks so he slowed down the ship and waved back. The beautiful lady made a gesture of welcome and the captain was captivated by her enchanting beauty without realizing that they were trudging on shallow waters and the propeller got entangled in the corals.

After being stuck for one day, the passengers and crew members went down to interact with the locals while the captain radioed their base. Two days after, a bigger boat fetched the passengers while the crew remained until a tug boat helped them pull the boat away.

A few years later, another ship ran aground on the coral reefs near the rock islet in Sitio Cantil. The captain apparently saw the same phenomenon and instead of the rock islet, he saw a pier where a beautiful woman was seductively waving to him and put him in a trance. The ship was stuck and was never removed from the place even with the help of powerful tugboats. Later on, the boat became a permanent fixture in the sea while corals have grown on its hull.

Bato was located along the feeder road to the town and was a popular picnic ground because it had white sand natural tide pools. The islet was accessible especially during low tide. Legend has it that the islet was formed after a fighting dog and cat were struck by lightning. Every time we passed by **Bato** on the way to town, Nanay would tell us the story. According to the legend, the cat and the dog were still fighting to this day and people can hear their noise every time it was raining.

There was a popular legend about our school being an enchanted place, it being a forested area before it became the Capul Agro Industrial School. People said that the developers and the *engkantos* had a truce in order to maintain peace in the campus: that a student would be sacrificed each year. Every time a student died, people thought they were taken to the netherworld hence they became *engkantos* themselves. Some people claimed they were seen frolicking with mermaids and nymphs in the brook that separates the Home Economics building from the rest of the campus. The residents inside the campus had myriad tales of unexplained occurrences especially at dusk or at night time. Our PE teacher allegedly saw elves playing by the flagpole at the Bermuda grass in front of the Vo-Ag building several times when she left her room after sundown. One *tambalan* even claimed that Elsa was among those living among the *englantos* in the campus.

Randy was a friend that we lost in junior year. I could not exactly remember how our friendship started and why we became close but he was friendly to everyone. Our female teachers adored him. His deep dimples and thick black hair that flipped when he danced made the girls swoon over him. He was sweet and had a ready smile for everyone. He would borrow my notes and scribble doodles on the back pages. He and his younger sister transferred from Manila to CAIS in our sophomore year after his mother unexpectedly died of cancer.

We did not know that he had a heart ailment because he was always cheerful and bubbly. He had a sunny disposition so we did not suspect that he was suffering from some illness, much more a terminal one. He even joined the officer training for CAT so we would go together to the training since he left his wooden rifle at home because his house was further in Zone Liang.

It was late December during the Christmas break when he was rushed to the hospital. He died shortly after. Everyone was in shock and in denial, especially our teachers. When the school opened in January, we visited him lying in state in their old house. He looked dapper in his long-sleeved barong and black pants. We wanted to believe that he was just playing some pranks to us like he sometimes did because we could not imagine him dead at fifteen. He was buried on my birthday near Elsa's grave. His father and younger sister were inconsolable.

Randy carried his playfulness until his death. As a class secretary, I was tasked to write the lesson on the board. A few days after he was buried, I heard his all-familiar voice.

"What word is that partly hidden by the curtain?"

I faced the class and saw him smiling naughtily at me, with his tongue out.

"Farming." I said, drawing the curtain to the sides and smiled back at him and continued writing, dusting the chalk dust from my hand.

Suddenly, I snapped back and remembered that he had died. When I looked again, there was only an empty chair where he used to sit. Several times, I caught his scent then a gash of cold air at our Chemistry class where we sat side by side. Our classmates also saw him in different parts of the room and inside the campus where he used to hang-out. One early morning, the girls saw him dancing on the stage while we were in formation at the quadrangle. The officers halted the training momentarily because the girls were crying and would not face the stage. We maintained his seat empty for the rest of the school year.

Chapter 22: Leaving the Island for the First Time

After living with my aunts, I decided to live at Tata Bala's house in my senior year in high school. This was a year after he died of old age and the house needed some serious repair. Dong and another cousin were also living in the house as well as Levi and later Beto, my classmate from Barangay Jubang. Living with my friends helped my anxiety and depression of losing Elsa. Even then, I could hear her voice randomly through my girlfriends when I felt down or was facing personal battles. I would visit her grave often and whisper to her as we passed by the public cemetery. I wondered how lonely she might be in her grave. I still dream about her and each time, her appearance changed like she aged with the times. I told her about my fears and apprehensions, my dreams and aspirations like we used to talk while walking to town on Sundays. She would listen and give me a piece of her mind like an older sister that she was. This continued even after college. Sometimes, I could hear her through Gonyang or Genith, two of my closest friends in college.

On Sundays, Beto brought ube from Jubang while Levi and I brought cassava or camote and coconut from San Luis so we had *ginat-an*. Friends would come over and the house was filled with laughter well into the night. Our neighbors would call us out when it was past bedtime. Some of our friends would sleep over so it was like a camp. Looking back, it was one of the most memorable moments of my young life even if it meant that I would go to school with an empty stomach. Because of it, I developed ulcer and migraine but it never diminished my tenacity. I decided firmly to continue my schooling no matter the odds. I thought of what I promised Elsa and I understood that I was my family's hope from then on. I remembered Nanay telling me that I should not rely on anyone, even my older siblings who were all married by now including Daria. Dong was helping Tatay on the farm full time after high school.

I tried participating in extracurricular activities like writing for the school paper and dancing with a group composed of my classmates although I sucked at modern dance. Besides, we were excused from participating in farming activities during rehearsals. I also tried running for the student body organization but I lost in the elections. Guess I was not really popular although some of my classmates asked for my help in writing their compositions. I enjoyed folk dancing and joined the literary-musical contests in school to overcome my shyness and lack of self-esteem. I was awkward and insecure because I wore the same clothes to school that I washed with the same laundry soap I used for my body, and shampoo was a luxury. I made do with the fifty pesos monthly allowance that I and the other top students received from Mr. Flores, a successful accountant working for SGV, the leading auditing firm based in Makati. It was released through the principal's office so there were times that I ate three square meals a day especially when it was released as a lump sum. Otherwise, I ate with my aunts or cousins who lived nearby.

In October of my senior year, six of my classmates left for Tacloban to take the UPCAT. It was the second time that I left the island; the first was a couple of months earlier when we had our photographs taken for the application forms. We went to Allen town because there are no photo studios on the island. Before that, I thought that any other place would look different from my island town so I was quite disappointed when I saw Allen for the first time. It looked like Capul! The difference was the presence of a pier where a couple of medium-sized passenger boats plying between Matnog and Allen were docked, four-wheeled automobiles in the dusty streets and few commercial establishments like small groceries, pharmacies, bakeshops, hard wares, plastic wares and the market all located in the same street and the availability of electricity, although we were told that it was often off. The photo studio was also located in the same street next to a carenderia adjacent to the church. We had to wait for two hours for the ID pictures to be developed so we waited at the churchyard looking out for the buses from Catarman that came every hour until past twelve. The houses near the pier were no different from my hometown. They had thatch roofs and walls and were obviously typhoon-battered. The houses at the town center were better-looking like the houses of the well-off families in Capul: bungalow or two-storied stone houses with corrugated tin roofs and porches facing the streets. The district hospital where Nanay's doctor-cousin worked was along the Maharlika Highway at the diversion road.

We took the 8:00 o'clock trip. On the way to Tacloban, I was wide awake during the more than six-hour land travel, memorizing the names of the towns and villages along the way by checking the markers and names of schools. I could hear the school children reciting their lessons and the teachers' voices dominating the classrooms. Most villages looked a lot like mine, the farmers and fishermen doing their daily chores, their nipa huts by the road side fenced with bamboo with chicken coop and a pig sty at the back while the children played in the river. The fathers carried rattan baskets of their produce on their backs with tattered shirts, mud caked on their bare feet. They smiled at the passing buses, showing the red stains on their teeth from chewing betel nuts. A few steps behind were the wives carrying baskets of vegetables and root crops while the older children carried firewood on their heads. Their farms were on the hills along the road, planted with taro, cassava, camote and beans on bamboo mango and pili trees planted on the edge of rice paddies being prepared for the next planting season. The farmers were tilling the land manually with a plough and harrow pulled by a carabao to overturn the soil, just like what Tatay and my older brothers were doing.

The Maharlika Highway snaked through the coastal communities traversing through the towns t and the lone city in Samar from the north to the southwest. We had a brief stopover in Calbayog City for lunch and in Catbalogan, the capital of Western Samar. The public parks in Calbayog and Catbalogan had students in uniform rehearsing dances while others chatted on the benches under the canopied trees. In Calbayog, I was captivated by a blind violinist playing Waray songs. Generous passengers gave him loose change and he would happily oblige for requests. I would encounter him every time the bus stops in Calbayog since then so I would reserve some loose change for him. A young girl, probably a grandchild, accompanied him in getting up and down the bus, thanking the passengers that clapped after his performance. He would play on all the buses that arrived every hour or so in that pit stop by the sea front.

We passed by markets with vendors peddling their wares, the fishmongers insisting that theirs was fresh showing the pinkish gills to anyone near, the meat sellers driving out the flies hovering around their hangers and the ambulant vegetable and root crops sellers silently sitting in corners arranging their merchandise in small clusters. Then there were the sellers of rice cakes, still warm from the charcoal-fired tin oven offering the passengers from passing buses on the windows. In Capul, pork and beef were only available on Sundays after the mass or on special occasions. The more enterprising vendors went up the buses every time we stopped and offered boiled eggs, soft drinks, peanuts and citrus fruits. I was content with boiled peanuts that I mindlessly shelled while looking out to the kaleidoscope of people and events unfolding outside the speeding bus. It was a never-ending pastoral scene of farms and rivers and the ocean on the other side until we came to the big towns.

At Jiabong, we were met by overeager vendors selling green mussels which were harvested on bamboo poles right at the mouth of the river. The bus slowed down so the vendors got inside the bus or called out from the open windows since it was not an official stop over. There were shelled tahong, tahong in bottles and tahong chips. Further in Calbiga, we passed by the *tabu* that started at midnight. Farmers offered freshly harvested Hawaiian pineapples, giant taro and varieties of bananas and plantains from their farms along the Calbiga River. I learned later during my research expeditions in the town that the *talyan* used in making *binagol, a delicacy* sold in Tacloban, were grown in upland communities in Calbiga as well as the *gaway* sold along with the *lechon* in Marasbaras district. Four years later, my team of fresh graduates from the university visited an upland village and joined the caravan at midnight to the river bank where the motorboats were waiting. We used torches made of dried coconut leaves to ward off snakes as we travelled downhill. The stillness of the night and the sparkle of the fireflies on the trees along the banks made it for a magical experience, the only sound was the hushed conversations of the farmers and the steady murmur of the engine. On the banks, the farmers would signal the passing boat by flashing light so that the boat was fully loaded of produce when it finally pulled up at the back of the market at the town. The motorboats came in from upstream and downstream bringing more products for the tabu. The middlemen were waiting for the producers of bananas and taro who will also sell the products in other towns and cities like Tacloban. On the other hand, the small producers sold their products themselves in the *tabu-an* until before lunchtime and buy their essentials like fish and salt before returning to their upland communities. Pigs and carabaos were slaughtered right at the market and sold along with fish caught from Catbalogan and Almagro. The *tabu* was done twice a week, on Thursdays and Sundays at the municipal market located right at the heart of the town. On Sundays, the men converged in the cockpit arena after selling their goods. In the olden times, the manner of exchange was mainly barter between the coastal and the upland communities.

When I saw the San Juanico Bridge for the first time, I excitedly patted my seatmate.

"Look, the San Juanico Bridge!"

I remembered the framed blown-up picture of our neighbor who have travelled to Tacloban in her youth. She was smiling, leaning on the rail while the buses speed along, the wind lapping on her face as she squinted to the camera. I thought the actual bridge was grander and longer than I imagined. From the signboard, I learned that the bridge was 2.162 kilometers long and connected the islands of Leyte and Samar.

"We are near Tacloban City." The bus conductor said, sensing my excitement.

I looked out the window with my hair licking on my face. The boats below looked like toys sailing in the narrow straight. It was on these waters that the biggest naval battle in modern history happened during World War II. The ships at the Tacloban harbor were visible from the bridge, the city skyline in the background.

We were met by an upperclassman at the bus terminal where we stayed in their boarding house in Pampango district. It was the semestral break so most of the rooms were vacant.

The following day, we checked our room assignment for the exam. The city I learned was not as imposing as I imagined it to be. Even UP Tacloban was not as splendid as the pictures of Diliman or Los Banos campuses, two of my other choices. I made Tacloban as my first choice of campus as advised by Gonyang since it would be difficult to qualify for the big campuses especially for quota courses that require higher GWA.

The UP Tacloban campus was composed of prefabricated buildings where students walked the distance between the Arts and Science and the BL campuses. The AS campus was where most of the general education subjects were located while the BL was for the business courses. The administration building and the library were located behind the Leyte Capitol building and was around one hundred meters away from AS and BL grounds so you had to specify to the tricycle driver which campus you were headed to. I was assigned to the multipurpose building at the Arts and Sciences campus together with other classmates while the others were assigned to the BL rooms.

Afterwards, we went to see the Botanical garden, the City Hall, Provincial Hall and the Children's park where we had our pictures taken.

The exam lasted for about three hours so I brought some crackers and bottled water. I did not expect to pass it because I was not familiar with some of the questions especially in grammar and Mathematics. We were instructed not to leave any item vacant so I made smart guesses on items that I was not sure of the answer. Probably it worked because I made it to the list of successful examinees which was released in March the following year.

We left Tacloban early the following morning. This time, I slept most of the way because we went to the disco house the night after the exam and woke up only during the stopover in Catbalogan.

In February of the following year, I also took the entrance exam at the University of Eastern Philippines where I qualified for the Veterinary

Medicine program. It was the first time that I saw for myself the campus where Mano Jun studied, more than fifteen years earlier. The first thing that impressed me was the sculpture of the water buffalo at the main entrance of the campus, the same image in the logo of my high school. Although Catarman is the capital of the province, some of the roads were not paved and were in fact dusty. The boarding houses inside the university town had no electricity and running water. I and another classmate stayed at my cousin's boarding house. The exam was not as overwhelming as the UPCAT.

When I was informed shortly before our graduation that I passed both the UPCAT and the UEPCAT, I had a fleeting excitement because I was unsure if I will continue to college knowing that my parents could hardly get things by.

On the day of my graduation, I wore a white long sleeved shirt that Nanay borrowed from a cousin. The black pants and black shoes were new, the shoes being a gift from Mano Jun while the pants were sewn by Nanay from a cloth that she bought from Mana Pilar's store. I got the third honors and was awarded best in English, Filipino, Social Studies and a special award as writer of the year owing to my being the editor-in-chief of the school paper. Nanay presented all my medals. It was a bitter-sweet moment knowing that I will not see some of my friends for a long time afterwards. Some of us will be studying in different schools while some will be working full-time for their families just like some of my classmates from elementary who did not continue to high school.

Chapter 23: The Last Fiesta

From the hill, the typhoon-battered thatch roofs looked like ruffled feathers. Some have patches of newly replaced nipa fronds while the more affluent families have tin roofs shining like silver in the summer sun. Ours leaked when it rained so we had to put pots and pails underneath. I would be awakened from my sleep in the middle of the night with my mat and blanket drenched in rainwater. The walls and windows were also made of pressed nipa fronds that we decorated with cut-out pictures from fashion magazines and calendars sent by my sisters in Manila.

The village was alive again. The scent of home-made coconut oil wafted through the air from the houses. Nanay and my sisters prepared *achara* a few days back for the fiesta. The basketball games were in full swing while the bannerettes were strung on the streets and in the coconut trees around the plaza. The *halu-halo* and fruit vendors were making a killing with the children and the adults buying every so often to soothe the summer heat. I wanted to memorize every nook and cranny of my village as I would be leaving after the fiesta.

Daria, Elsa and I took turns in pounding rice in the wooden mortar. We needed to polish as much so we had enough even after the fiesta. Tatay has collected a few containers of coconut wine from his own *sanggutan* for his guests. In the backyard, we have stacked firewood and charcoal for cooking.

Until this time, I have not received my admission slip from UP so I was worried that I would not be able to enroll. When I inquired at the principal's office, I was told that the guidance counsellor who was in-charge was on leave and had not sent my grades to the university. I was disheartened and I thought that my chances for the scholarship were already nil. It was the second week of April and I needed to submit all the other requirements for incoming freshmen by May as they were also on the wait-list.

My parents could not send me to UEP either because they could not afford the expenses that will cover my living expenses. The tuition fee was surely low but they could not afford the board and lodging expenses with their unsteady income. The coconuts were still recovering from the typhoons the previous year. It would take at least two years for the trees to recover, granting that there was no new strong typhoon by the middle of the year when the monsoons started. My admission to UP would also guarantee full scholarship through the Socialized Tuition and Financial Assistance Program as long as I maintained a passing grade every semester. To qualify, I have to submit a certification from the barangay that my parents were in fact indigent, having no fixed income and did not possess any real property except our house which was Tatay's only inheritance from Tata Iling. We had to update its tax declaration too to get a certificate from the assessor's office that it did cost much being built of light materials and measured less than a hundred square meters. Gonyang guided us through the process of completing the requirements. The only missing was the admission slip from the university so I can go ahead with the enrolment.

The fiesta came and went like a blur. For me it will be the last one before I leave for Manila with Baba Monding, who will help me look for a job. Baba Monding came with his family as a thanksgiving for his daughter for surviving a life threatening illness so we went around all the chapels in the island, travelled on foot to most of the villages because there were no access roads at this time between the villages. Cathy was hospitalized for a long time the previous year and Baba Monding promised to go home once she survived. In Manila, I will have to work my way to college as a working student so I may not be able to go home even on fiestas.

"Just like my older siblings." I thought.

June came but no notice arrived so in the second week, I finally resolved to leave for Manila. On the last day before my trip, Levi and I went out gathering mussels beneath the lighthouse. Levi will be leaving too with his sister later in the week. The other *balikbayans* left days after the fiesta so the village was quiet once again. The farmers were waiting for the first monsoon rains for the *habagat* season so they could start preparing the fields and the seedlings. The summer heat was still raging so the last of the late harvest were dried and winnowed in the sun while the farmer whistled for the breeze to come. The women fanned themselves while having their siesta in hammocks in their veranda, while the men were shirtless and sprawled on wooden benches in almost complete abandon. The seas were calm and I could see the tip of the Mayon volcano from faraway Albay while Mt. Bulusan was looming in front of us from across the sea like a giant threatening to attack anytime. The M/V Maharlika passed by with loads of passengers and vehicles crossing the San Bernardino Strait from Matnog to San Isidro port in mainland Samar, then to Leyte and the islands of Mindanao. People move around, leaving and returning to peoples and places. Who knows where they were going and to whom were they returning to? On moonless nights, the lighthouse would serve as a beacon to ships and travelers finding their way in the dark.

We have gathered enough and walked leisurely home, savoring the moment as we may not see each other again soon. I would be staying in Las Pinas while Levi would be based in Cavite. We talked about anything and everything that caught our attention along the way. We would have wanted to wait for the lighting of the *parola* but it would be dark soon and there was a portion in the road that we feared because of the big trees near a creek which according to unverified sources were the exit from the tunnels from beneath the lighthouse. Supposedly, the Japanese dug the tunnels during the Second World War as a hiding place.

Nanay was winnowing and cleaning the rice when I returned home, the leftover of the fiesta which I assumed was for my trip to Manila.

"You are leaving tomorrow."

"So Baba Danding finally decided to return to Manila tomorrow?"

"No, for Tacloban. Your Tatay will accompany you. Look, the letter came today." Nanay handed me the already open letter. My hands were trembling with anticipation when I saw the return address.

"This is my admission slip! It finally arrived!" I exclaimed and jumped for joy.

"Pack your things now so you don't forget anything."

Nanay gave me two thousand pesos that she borrowed from a relative. She will pay for it plus a twenty percent interest in the next three months so the money should last me until the month of August or until the first stipend will be released. Every time I need money before the regular release of the stipend, Nanay would borrow money from relatives who will be charging twenty percent interest from the principal amount so I have to think of it before I buy things that might be considered a luxury. I gathered the documents for the STFAP and packed my best clothes which could fit into a small backpack. That night, I laid awake for a long time trying to believe that I was going away to college. It will be the first time that I will be living away from home so I will be on my own although I will be sharing the room with other students from my hometown which was also a new experience for me. My parents were talking in whispers in the other room arguing how they could support my college education in a faraway city.

"The coconuts do not always bear many fruits. Sometimes the copra sells very low. . ." Tatay sighed and could not finish his sentence, probably thinking about the still emaciated trees. Some trees were completely destroyed from the previous typhoon like burnt candles so they have to be replaced.

"We can manage. I will sell more mats and cook viands so we can send Alex a little money." Nanay was sure of what to do even then. She would sell cooked vegetables or *paksiw* to our neighbors when she was not weaving mats, sometimes even travelling to other villages like Ilawod and to sell or barter fish with rice grains. I used to go with her when I was ten years old and I would carry home whatever I could on my skinny back, navigating the hilly and sometimes slippery dirt road. We would sell the rice to local traders or barter them with fish from San Vicente or Ticao islands. If it was the season for anchovies, Nanay would make dried fish cakes from the fries that the local fishermen caught with hand nets in the bay at dusk. The fish cakes can last up to a month and are best cooked in coconut milk and *malunggay* leaves.

"What if there's another typhoon, where do we get money if there is no copra?" Tatay's voice was hushed but worried knowing that I might be listening in the other room. My brother Jonas was sleeping on the floor next to my bag. The quarter sack of polished rice that I was bringing was in the living room packed inside an empty carton of Tanduay, labelled with my name and tied with straw. Inside were also a few kilos of dried sardines that would last me at least a couple of weeks.

"Our son is determined to go to college so we have to support him in any way we can." Nanay was firm and determined.

"I hope he will not do what Jun did. . ."

"Let us give him a chance. I believe Alex is different."

I touched my bag and shoes to ensure that they were under my bed. I laid awake long after the kerosene lamp was extinguished. A firefly sparkled on the roof like some distant dying star. I gazed at it, mesmerized by its blinking luminescent light as it flitted along the roof. At one time, it flew so low that I wanted to catch it in my hands until I fell asleep.

Nanay woke me up at five o'clock. My bath and breakfast were ready. Nanay went ahead to the chapel to say the rosary while Tatay was having his coffee and breakfast ahead of me. He had bathed. Tatay wanted to accompany me to Tacloban for my enrollment and probably to see where I stayed so he could visit me should the need be. He was probably thinking about Mano Jun and the first time he went away from the university. He was silent the whole time.

Nanay touched my head and then the rest of my body with the image of De Salvacion while praying for my safety during my travels. She prayed for my protection while I was away in the city. I kissed the feet of the little Jesus while praying on my own, asking for strength and perseverance while I was away from home. My cousin drove us to the dock in the poblacion. I murmured a prayer for Elsa to help me in my journey while we passed by the municipal cemetery.

The boat was loaded with students returning to the universities in Catarman, Calbayog, Catbalogan and Tacloban. Those going to Manila were in another motor boat that had departed ahead of us going to

Matnog. I was with my classmate Dennis who was also with his father to enroll in the Catholic university in Tacloban. Dennis was one of the first who befriended me in high school. Sometimes, he would take me home on his bike on Friday afternoons. Dennis will be taking up Criminology to become a policeman just like his father. I was not sure what courses were still open because it was already late. In fact, it was the last day of the late enrolment in the state university when I enrolled on that Monday of June 17, 1991.

The bus from Catarman was almost full when it passed by Allen. It was a good thing that some passengers dropped off so we were able to get seats at the back. More passengers contented themselves standing at the aisle. Tatay and I glanced at the house of Dada Titay when we passed by Tangolon hoping to see her but she was probably working at the farm. Just like the first time, I was awake during the six hours of travel to Tacloban. A lot of things were on my mind, foremost of which was to survive the city life and student life away from my family. The six-hour bus ride was interrupted every now and then by potholes on the road and by alighting and loading passengers at the junctions. I could see that most of them were students returning to the universities, their oversized bags on their backs and another box of provisions, probably rice and dried fish from their hometowns that they put on the side container of the bus.

It was past two o'clock when we passed by the San Juanico Bridge. Giant billboards on the side of the highway announced the upcoming fiesta and *pintados* festival which will happen at the end of the month. Arches and colorful banners decorated the entrances of the villages. Children played on the side roads while the older people chatted in front of the stores.

The city was even livelier as we navigated the rather narrow road going to the terminal. The strong stench coming from the wet market nearby made me nauseous. Billboards and tarpaulins sponsored by big business establishments lined the streets, plastered on the buildings and hung on the lampposts with images of the *pintados* and the Sto. Nino, the patron saint of Tacloban. Heavy traffic of jeepneys and tricycles ply the streets along with private vehicles. On the sidewalks were vendors selling shirts, towels and fruits and people probably negotiating for better bargains. The conductor reminded us to mind our belongings after alighting the bus, especially from those offering help.

Before alighting from the bus, I took the small piece of paper from my pocket that Nanay gave me before I left the house. There was a small amount of sand from our front door. I took it out and stepped on it.

"To take away the homesickness and for you to find a new home away from home." Her voice reverberated in my head.

-------- **END** --------

About the Author

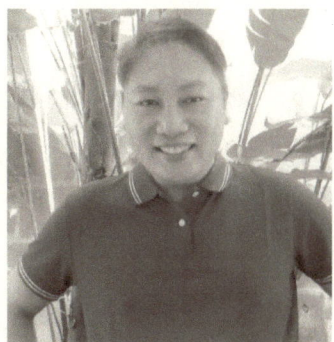

Alex M. Castillo

Alex has been writing short stories, poems and essays since his high school days. One of his short story for children was awarded first prize for a nationwide contest sponsored by the National Book Development Board-Philippines and his poems was included in the anthology of the best works of Lamiraw Literary Workshop. He finished a Bachelor of Arts in Communication Arts at the University of the Philippines Tacloban College and is currently working as a government employee. He writes in both English and Inabaknon, his mother tongue.

www.ingramcontent.com/pod-product-compliance
Lightning Source LLC
LaVergne TN
LVHW041609070526
838199LV00052B/3056